PRAISE FOR *FAULT LINES*

'A cracking and highly original thriller. Johnstone never fails to deliver' Mark Billingham

'You don't read *Fault Lines* so much as you white-knuckle your way through its twists and turns, toward its thrilling end, your breath held and your nerves tingling. And it's as psychologically rich as it is harrowing. I've come to expect nothing less from Doug Johnstone, one of the genre's premiere writers' Megan Abbott

'Doug Johnstone has crafted a superb, highly original psychological chiller. *Fault Lines* is a masterclass in suspense' Steve Cavanagh

'Doug Johnstone is a brilliant writer and this is a pacey, gripping read, which builds to a climax you won't forget in a hurry. Loved it' Louise Voss

'Doug Johnstone is Scotland's truest exponent of noir. He writes novels that are punchy, fast paced and sometimes gruellingly dark; unflinchingly challenging his readers by taking them to places that are emotionally and ideologically uncomfortable' Chris Brookmyre

'A subtly off-kilter speculative thriller that builds to a truly explosive ending. Once again Doug Johnstone shows why he's at the forefront of Scottish crime fiction's new guard; *Fault Lines* is original, ambitious but always grounded in relatable and complex characters' Eva Dolan

'*Fault Lines* creates a world so convincing you find yourself forgetting it is a work of fiction. Richly characterised, beautifully crafted, this is a book that you truly inhabit. A true must read' Emma Kavanagh

'Sexy, fearless and addictive – *Fault Lines* isn't like any other book I've read. Doug Johnstone just gets better and better' Helen FitzGerald

'In Surtsey, Doug Johnstone has created a character as feisty and unpredictable as the volcano that has transformed the Firth of Forth. Johnstone weaves his compelling and original tale with great skill and elegance from the gripping beginning to a tense and explosive end' Amanda Jennings

'Doug Johnstone is one of this country's finest, and bravest, thriller writers. *Fault Lines* is brilliantly unputdownable' Martyn Waites

'I'm a massive fan of Doug Johnstone's books and *Fault Lines* does not disappoint. From its chilling opening to its explosive ending, this is a thriller not to be missed. Superb!' Luca Veste

'In *Fault Lines*, Doug Johnstone manages the rare feat of bringing something truly original to the crime genre. Blending powerful imagination and plotting, this is the work of a writer at the top of his game' Stuart Neville

Fault Lines

Doug Johnstone is an author, journalist and musician based in Edinburgh. He's had eight previous novels published, most recently *Crash Land*. His novel, *The Jump*, was a finalist for the McIlvanney Prize for Scottish Crime Novel of the Year. Several of his other novels have been award winners and bestsellers, and he's had short stories published in numerous anthologies and literary magazines. His work has been praised by the likes of Ian Rankin, Val McDermid and Irvine Welsh. Several of his novels have been optioned for film and television.

Doug is also a Royal Literary Fund Consultant Fellow. He's worked as an RLF Fellow at Queen Margaret University, taught creative writing at Strathclyde University and been Writer in Residence at both Strathclyde University and William Purves Funeral Directors. He mentors and assesses manuscripts for The Literary Consultancy and regularly tutors at Moniack Mhor writing retreat. Doug has released seven albums in various bands, and is the drummer for the Fun Lovin' Crime Writers, a band of crime writers. He also reviews books for *The Big Issue* magazine, is player-manager for Scotland Writers Football Club and has a PhD in nuclear physics.

Follow him on Twitter @doug_johnstone and visit his website: dougjohnstone.com.

Fault Lines

Doug Johnstone

ORENDA BOOKS

Orenda Books
16 Carson Road
West Dulwich
London SE21 8HU
www.orendabooks.co.uk

First published in the United Kingdom by Orenda Books, 2018
Copyright © Doug Johnstone 2017

A catalogue record for this book is available from the British Library.

ISBN 978-1-912374-15-1
eISBN 978-1-912374-16-8

Typeset in Garamond by MacGuru Ltd
Printed and bound by Nørhaven, Denmark

For sales and distribution, please contact *info@orendabooks.co.uk*

For Andrew and Eleanor

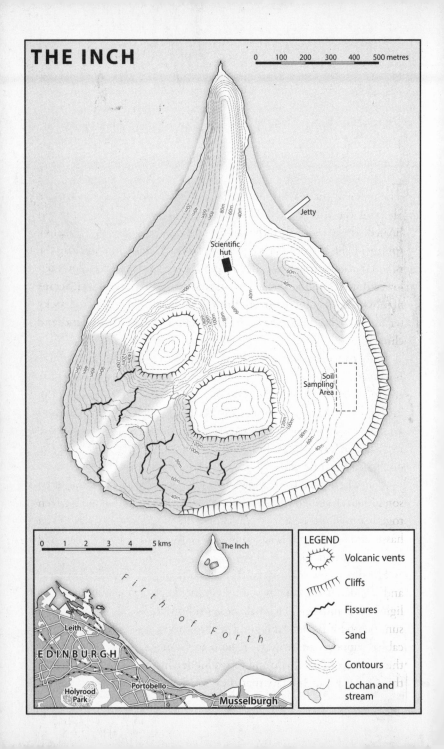

THE INCH

0 100 200 300 400 500 metres

Jetty

Scientific hut

Soil Sampling Area

80m 60m 40m
100m
40m
60m
40m
100m
80m
140m
120m
100m
60m
40m
80m
120m
120m
100m
80m
60m
40m
80m
60m
40m
20m

0 1 2 3 4 5 kms

The Inch

F i r t h   o f   F o r t h

Leith

EDINBURGH

Holyrood Park

Portobello

Musselburgh

LEGEND

Volcanic vents

Cliffs

Fissures

Sand

Contours

Lochan and stream

1

The moment she set foot on the Inch she felt something was wrong. She tied the three-seater RIB to a mooring post on the jetty and turned. The island looked the same, black sand shimmering in the low summer light, the sun's rays bouncing down the Forth and hitting the island in a low-slung blaze. Beyond the beach hardened lava flows billowed down from the volcanic vents that dominated the island. Scraps of moss and sea grass cut green through the black and grey of the rocky terrain, over the years they'd brought life to the newborn land and clung on.

It was too quiet, Surtsey realised, that was the problem. Where were the gulls and crows? Scientists had been coming to the island since it emerged in a giant plume of volcanic ash twenty-five years ago. The birds knew that humans meant possible food and usually greeted their arrival with a flurry of squawks and shrieks. But she was alone, just the low ruffle of waves on the beach, the hollow thud of her rigid-hull boat bobbing against the jetty.

And where was Tom's boat? He didn't always moor at the jetty, sometimes he landed round the coast, paranoid about them being seen together even out here in the middle of the firth. But that was such a hassle and he'd been relaxed about it recently, so Surtsey was surprised not to see it tied up.

She did a slow three-sixty, the salty bite of the sea air in her nose, and wondered what she was missing. Inchkeith to the northwest, its lighthouse and derelict battlements silhouetted against the setting sun. Behind it Burntisland and the three bridges, a mess of struts and cables, supports and towers. Round to Granton and Leith harbour, the beaches of Portobello and Joppa hidden by the island's peaks from this side. It was deliberate that they met on the north side, in case of prying eyes with strong binoculars. Surtsey looked up at the twin volcanic peaks, brooding in the dusk. Surtsey had been up those slopes, explored every scrap of the Inch over many visits since she began her studies. So lucky to be a volcanologist and have this on her doorstep, the best laboratory in the world with Edinburgh University leading research.

She looked to the east, the flat expanse of East Lothian. She got a flutter of unease at the missing Cockenzie power station chimneys. They'd been a landmark of her childhood in Joppa, and their recent demolition left a flicker of longing in her heart. Further east was Berwick Law then open sea, tankers drifting out there, wash glittering in the light.

Where was he?

She checked her phone. No new message, just the text from earlier:

Fancy a picnic tonight? Usual time and place. Tx

'Picnic' was a stupid euphemism, Tom trying to be careful. Unnecessary, since it was from the phone he only used for her, the phone his wife didn't know about.

It had been going on for six months. The first time was after a drinks thing at uni, celebrating a new grant award for the research group, money that would keep everyone coming back to the Inch for years. After cheap Prosecco in the Grant Institute at King's Buildings a handful of them moved on to beers at The Old Bell. Surtsey was drunk enough to flirt with him and to be flattered by his attention. He was twenty years older and married, but he was sharp, had authority and a certain charm, still handsome and trim. And he was ridiculously grateful, one reason she kept it going, the look in his eyes when she undressed in front of him. He was getting to fuck a firm twenty-five year old for the first time since his wife had been that age, and he was like an excitable puppy. It was so different to sex with Brendan, ages with her, cute and skinny, innocent and uncomplicated.

She hit reply on her phone:

I'm here. Where r u? x

She walked off the jetty and jumped onto the beach. Even though she knew the geological processes that made it she was still amazed by the black sand, glistening like oil where it was wet, more like iron filings above high tide. She lifted a handful and let it run through her fingers, then brushed her hand on her dress. She wasn't really a summer dress kind of person, vest tops and jeans usually, but she like to play the young ingénue with Tom, actually enjoyed the stereotype. They both realised the cliché of the situation, older academic having an affair with young PhD student. Surtsey imagined she was in a Richard Curtis film or a corny novel by some middle-aged Oxbridge guy.

There were no footprints in the sand. That didn't necessarily mean anything, Tom could've landed round the coast and come over the ridge. But something about the blankness of the sand unnerved her. And the birds, where were the birds?

She walked up the beach onto the patchy grass and called him. She wasn't supposed to do that even though he kept it on silent, but something didn't feel right.

Maybe he got caught up with Alice and the kids at home, unable to make excuses. That went with the territory, of course. He wouldn't have just forgotten, that wasn't like him. One of the things Surtsey liked about their set-up was that she was at the forefront of his mind throughout the day. She liked that compared to Brendan, who occasionally treated her like an afterthought.

The phone went to voicemail. She didn't leave a message.

She walked round the coast towards the scientific hut, its white walls and blue corrugated roof stark against the black landscape. The hut was little more than a bothy with a bed, some basic lab and storage equipment, and a stove in the corner. He wasn't likely to be there, they never used it, scared of leaving a trace that other department members would find. They always chose somewhere outdoors but sheltered, on their own little island paradise only a couple of miles from Edinburgh. That was part of this whole thing, their shared love of the Inch, the violence of its creation, its settling and erosion, the spread of life across it. An Eden for them to share.

Surtsey had been obsessed with the place her whole life. Just as the Inch was being spewed from the bowels of the earth, a new volcanic island created from an unknown fault line in the Firth of Forth, Surtsey's mum was in the back of a taxi on the way to the old Royal to give birth to her. Hence the weird name, Louise naming her daughter after another new island born from the sea, the Icelandic island she'd visited as a young volcanologist herself.

Surtsey was at the hut now. She hesitated with her hand at the door then swallowed and pushed it open.

Empty. A blanket stretched across the bed, the stove cold, equipment untouched.

She left and looked around again. Further west was a rise in the rock, dipping down to a small cove. A seagull came out of the darkening sky, a bluster of wings, then landed out of sight behind the mound.

Surtsey walked towards it, her stomach tight. She checked her phone again, no message. She picked her way over the cracked surface, careful in her Converse. She liked the way the trainers looked with the dress, made her feel less prim.

As she approached the edge of the lava flow two crows burst up from behind it, cawing and flapping, a flurry of black feathers. They descended behind the bank, out of sight again.

Surtsey reached the edge of the outcrop. Thirty yards below, on the sand of the cove, a dozen gulls and crows were gathered on a single low rock, a blur of squawking activity, pecking at each other. Surtsey watched for a few moments trying to make sense of it. Gradually she realised they weren't pecking each other, they were pecking at the rock beneath them.

Then she got it.

It wasn't a rock it was a body, and they were feasting on it.

2

She looked around as if someone might appear with an answer. She scanned the horizon for any activity apart from the chaos of birds. Nothing. The air was full of caws and screeches and she couldn't concentrate. She looked at her phone then back at the birds.

She picked her way down the rocky escarpment, sharp stones jabbing the soles of her shoes. Her dress snagged on a ragged edge and she pulled it free. She felt hot, blood in her cheeks with the effort.

The sound of the birds grew louder as she got nearer, the tussle at the beach in full flow, gulls lifting into the air then settling back down. Surtsey saw clothing, a light jacket, jeans, brown shoes. Clothes she thought she recognised. The birds were concentrating on the exposed head and hands, where they could get better purchase.

She stumbled onto the sand, the birds ignoring her, but as she walked closer the nearest crows began shuffling away from her. She hesitated, hand to her mouth. She looked back up the way she'd come, then out to sea. The sun was setting now, just a few strands of pink between the slats of the bridges in the distance. It was still light, though, would be for a couple of hours yet at this time of year.

She turned back to look at the body. She was twenty yards away. She saw a seagull pick something from the face, flap up into the air chased by two others. It evaded them, switched back beyond high tide and landed, pulling whatever it was between its beak and feet.

Surtsey's stomach lurched. Acid rose from her stomach, but she swallowed it down. She took a breath and strode towards the body, waving her hands, shooing the birds away, clapping and shouting. They flustered into the sky but didn't go too far, circling above her, a mass of black and white darting and skipping through the air, eyeing her.

She stood over the body and felt another rush of blood, heart clattering in her ribs, fingers tingling.

Tom.

She closed her eyes, kept them closed for a long time.

She opened them and looked away, up at the vents towering above her, over at the spread of dried lava tumbling down the hillside from them. Out to sea. Then eventually she turned back to his body, made herself look.

His head was caved in on the right hand side, blood soaking the sand and making it shine. His scalp was a mess of skin, bone and hair on that side, his ear mangled and hanging off, eyebrow collapsed, cheekbone flat. His eyes stared up at the sky.

She'd seen those eyes earlier today back at the office, glancing at her in a team meeting, something passing between them, a little spark. Nothing profound, just a look.

She fell to her knees, felt the roughness of the sand on her skin. She thought about Alice, the girls. How would they cope? She thought about the reaction in the department, the professor no longer there to guide them.

She reached out to touch his hand but hesitated. The wedding ring, a simple platinum band. He never hid it or took it off when they were together, and she'd never asked him to.

Above her the crows and gulls suddenly stopped fighting and flew higher into the sky. She put her hands to her face, covered her eyes. Sat on her knees for a moment, then felt a vibration, subsonic, a sensation she recognised. It grew stronger and the sand shuffled around her knees. She felt a ripple through her body from the land beneath. An earthquake, a pretty strong one. She tried to get up but a judder pitched her forward and she rested her hand on Tom's chest for balance. She pushed up and eased herself to her feet, spread her weight as she'd been taught, looked at the gulls way overhead. The ground kept shuddering, no rhythm to it, creaks and tilts. Even though she'd lived a lifetime with them, she never got used to it. She tried to imagine a time before the Inch, before the new fault line had opened up, when Scotland never had an earthquake worth mentioning. But it seemed impossible, they were as much a part of life as breathing.

The world trembled on, vibrations in her legs, thrumming in her pelvis and womb, her stomach, spreading up her spine. There was a lurch to the right and she stumbled, caught herself. She heard a ripping noise from above and saw a cascade of small boulders tumbling from the side of the vents, clattering down the rock face, kicking up grit and dirt as they rolled, then settling a few hundred yards away.

She was OK, that's what she kept telling herself. Unless the earth actually opened up and swallowed her right here on the beach, she was safe. It was buildings you had to watch for. That and tsunamis, but they'd never had one here yet in twenty-five years, and while this quake was sizeable it wasn't the biggest she'd experienced.

The throb beneath her feet began to ebb away, echoing down into the mantle, the earth settling back. The whole thing had lasted maybe thirty seconds. She wondered what number it was on the scale.

Then she thought of Tom. Alice and the girls. And herself. The slut, the mistress. The home wrecker.

The silence after the quake was ominous, forbidding.

If she called the police she would have to explain what she was doing here, what Tom was doing here. Then it would all come out. His wife and family. Her mum, Brendan. Everyone would know.

She spotted something in the sand beyond his right hand. The old Nokia, the phone he used just for her. She looked around at the shore, wondered where his boat was. The birds were returning, getting closer above her head. She picked up his phone and stared at it, wiped it on her dress to get the sand off. She felt ridiculous in this dress now, a piece of fakery. She had been living a lie with Tom.

She looked at him.

'Sorry,' she said, and started walking back towards the jetty.

3

The spray from the prow dampened her dress and felt like a slap in the face. She closed her eyes and gave herself over to the salty tang of the sea stinging her skin. The outboard motor was at full throttle, the whine of the engine filling her ears as the boat bucked over the waves. She headed east towards the widening mouth of the firth, refusing to look at the island behind or the coastline to either side. If she kept going all the way to Scandinavia she would never have to deal with any of it.

The motor strained and she became aware of the clamour of it out here on the empty water. She cut the engine and the silence pressed down on her, the slap of wave on hull the only sound. She sat for a long time listening to that noise, trying to find a pattern in it, but it was disjointed and random.

Eventually she turned back to the Inch. It looked like a cancerous growth on the skin of the water, the two volcanic lumps of the vents rippling down to the stark southeastern cliffs. The northern beach and jetty were invisible from here. The same for the cove where Tom lay.

She looked south to Joppa and Portobello. The sun had set but the sky was still eerily bright, that unsettling paradox of Scottish summertime. In this light the beach seemed smeared across the land, thick painted brushstrokes in front of the precise sketch lines of the houses behind.

She tried to pick out her own place from the row of low tenements at the eastern end of the shoreline. Some lights coming on in the front rooms, but she couldn't see which was hers. She wondered if Halima was in the kitchen knocking together something spicy with a large glass of Rioja in her hand. Or Iona, throwing clothes around trying to decide what to wear for tonight's shift. People she loved going about their lives. She stared at the stumpy, flat-roofed houses and wished she was inside, sharing department gossip with Halima or shouting at Iona to pick up after herself.

She looked at the bigger Victorian properties along the prom. She could pick out St Columba's easily with the observation tower poking up from the sprawl of dark stone. Her mum would be there. She was diminishing every day, retreating from the world one breath at a time. So much life reduced to a bag of bones, half her stomach cut away, growths in her pelvis and liver, tangled up her spine. Only a matter of time.

Surtsey thought about Tom. She pictured his slender fingers on her hips that first time, a reassuring touch to her elbow in the office, his goofy smile whenever she walked into the room.

She'd been pushing them away but now the thoughts slipped in. How had it happened? Maybe he fell and hit his head. But where was his boat? It could be moored beyond the cove, but why do that? If his boat wasn't there, that meant someone else had taken it or it had drifted away. If someone else took it, how had they got to the island themselves, where was their boat? Did they come with Tom, was it someone he knew? Was it murder?

Maybe he fell and hit his head on a rock, staggered forward onto the beach. The hardened tephra and palagonite tuff were razor sharp in places, an edge to the wrong part of your head and you'd be in trouble. She hadn't examined his wound closely, hadn't looked around for rocks or boulders, too keen to escape.

It must be lonely back there on the island. When eventually it got dark in the early hours and the wind picked up along the Forth, he would need a blanket to keep warm. Stupid thoughts, chewing her up.

She trailed a hand in the water, cold against her fingers, and shivered as a breeze stirred around her.

Too quiet, too much time to think. She needed to be moving, active.

She started the engine and pointed the boat towards shore, opened the throttle and picked up speed, flecks of spray in her face. She opened her mouth and tasted the salt.

She was at the east end of Portobello beach in ten minutes. She angled the prow alongside the last groyne and drove the boat as close as she could, then cut the engine, flipped off her shoes and jumped out, pulling the boat in on the towrope. She heaved it onto the trailer she'd left sitting in the wash and fastened it, then hauled the whole thing up the sand to the gap in the low seawall, then onto the prom.

Her muscles burned as she pulled the boat and trailer round the back of Esplanade Terrace onto the cobbles of Joppa Park. She stopped at the back of her house and opened the boatshed doors, wheeled the trailer inside. She was panting as she dropped the trailer handle, hands on her knees, bent over to get her breath back. Eventually she stood up. From the small, cobwebbed window of the shed she could see into the kitchen at the back of the house. Halima was there, drinking and cooking, just as she had pictured.

Surtsey grabbed a towel off a nail stuck in the wall and dried her face, hair and arms, then dabbed at the front of her dress. She left the shed and went back out into the street, closing the door as quietly as she could.

She stood breathing for a few moments, trying to get her heart to slow, then lifted the latch on the back gate and walked through, clattering it shut behind her. When she turned round Halima was smiling from the kitchen, already pouring a glass of red wine for her.

4

'Hey, babes, you're back early.' Halima handed the wine to Surtsey before she was even through the sliding doors. Surtsey tried to keep her hand steady as she took it, then had three gulps, almost finishing the glass.

Halima smiled. 'Date didn't go well, huh?'

Surtsey shook her head. To cover for her and Tom over the last few months she'd sold Halima a line about trying online dating behind Brendan's back. Since she and Halima lived and worked together, she needed something to explain her absences, and that was the perfect cover story. It made Halima into a co-conspirator with Surtsey, gave them a secret they shared, and made sure she wouldn't ever blurt it out to anyone. Plus she knew Halima wouldn't judge her.

'So who was this dick?'

'Just a hipster in a folk band. Loved himself.'

'His loss.'

Halima wandered over to the stove where a pot of something was simmering. It smelt spicy and sweet and Surtsey felt hungry, then disgusted with her body for carrying on regardless.

'Ready in ten minutes,' Halima said. 'Get yourself settled and we can have a boozy night in.' She waved her glass, the wine almost spilling over the side. 'Drink our troubles away.'

Surtsey finished her wine then filled both of them up from the bottle.

'Sounds great,' she said.

*

The stainless steel hash pipe seemed to glow as Halima handed it to her. It was the size of a credit card, small bowl at one end, fern leaf engraved along the edge. It was Halima's twenty-first birthday present from her mum and dad. The Maliks didn't conform to the strict Muslim parent stereotype, second-generation Scots-Pakistani hippies who ran a drop-in centre for troubled teens in Glasgow and grew asparagus and courgettes on their allotment.

The warmth of the pipe in Surtsey's hand sent a tingle along her fingers. She sparked the lighter, held the flame to the grass in the bowl and took a hit. The crackle of burning grass and the gas fizzing in the Zippo filled her brain. She felt thirsty and took a careful gulp of Shiraz, then placed her glass down and handed the pipe back.

'I'm wrecked,' Halima giggled.

'Yep.'

The news was on television in the corner of the living room. Surtsey blinked and looked round. All her mum's stuff still here, despite the fact she didn't live here any more. The whitewashed wooden book-shelves full of geophysics and earth science books, the saggy brown leather sofas, the worn Indonesian rug on the floorboards, the out-of-tune piano against the back wall. And the Celestron telescope set up in the bay window, pointing at the Inch. Surtsey had used it earlier today before she left for her rendezvous. She stared at it now.

She turned and tried to focus on the photographs lining the mantel-piece. Her graduation picture in that stupid gown next to a snapshot of Iona taken when she didn't realise, the only way Louise could catch her younger daughter on camera in the last few years. Then a holiday photo of the three of them squinting into the sun at Pompeii, Louise's idea of a fun family trip, traipsing around hundreds of mummified people killed by a volcanic explosion.

She tried not to think about Tom on the island. She should've found a blanket for him, taken the bedding from the hut, kept him cosy against the wind.

'What you thinking about?' Halima said.

Her voice seemed to come from the bottom of a well.

Surtsey took in Halima's glossy black hair, dark eyes, sly smile. They'd been best friends since freshers' week six years ago, meeting on a dumb Geosoc pub crawl down Cowgate and immediately clicking, bunking off halfway and pitching up at a shitty dive on Niddrie Street, an old man's pub with bright strip lights, stuffed animals on the gantry and empty ashtrays still on the table.

At first they bonded over mockery of the straighter students on the course, but that acerbic fluff gradually gave way to something deeper, a shared understanding of the importance of friendship and family. Hal was the youngest of six siblings and was forever heading off in a bright sari to some cousin's wedding or aunt's birthday, rolling her eyes at the conformity but also revelling in it. We all live multiple lives, Surtsey thought, play different roles as a daughter, friend, student, lover.

Surtsey remembered that Halima had asked a question.

'Mum,' she said.

'Oh, babes.' Halima reached over and touched Surtsey's hair. She ran a finger around the edge of her ear and Surtsey shivered, then she touched Surtsey's loop earring, a tiny tug that pulled at the lobe.

Now Surtsey really was thinking about her mum. They'd spent three years apart when Surtsey left school, the usual quest for independence. Surtsey split rent with Halima on a crappy student flat in Sciennes, five minutes from the action of George Square. But Louise got the diagnosis at the start of Surtsey's final year and she moved back in to help out, tearful at first but some laughs along the way, Iona storming around as if their mum dying was a personal affront, something she still did. Surtsey could understand that anger, God knows she felt it too, but in the end what good did it do?

Six months ago, with Louise deteriorating fast, they managed to get a place in the hospice five minutes up the road. Surtsey didn't have it in her to keep changing grown-up nappies, cleaning up sick and helping her mum to the toilet. Louise hated all that too, ashamed of being babied by her own daughter. Through all this, Iona kept stomping around refusing to accept, a human storm cloud rumbling through life.

So this house was Surtsey and Iona's home now, and Halima was here too having moved in partly to keep Surtsey company, partly because it was rent free. Louise was never coming home, that was the truth. The only way she was leaving the hospice was in a wooden box. Surtsey felt sick thinking about it.

She stared at the television, her stoned brain sucked into the glow of it. It was a news story about the earthquake earlier. 5.7 on the scale, no real damage done, a few minor aftershocks, a warning about future tremors. They were so used to it now it was barely worth mentioning unless it was a really big one.

She wondered what time it was. They'd been drinking and smoking for hours, watching *Kimmy Schmidt*, *Parks & Rec*, old *30 Rock*.

Surtsey frowned and pushed herself up from the sofa. It took enormous effort, muscles straining. She stumbled over to the telescope and bent to look through the eyepiece.

Halima laughed. 'What are you doing? It's dark, you can't see anything.'

Surtsey kept her eye to the telescope, staring at the blackness.

5

Surtsey was too wired from the grass to sleep, lying in bed imagining she was in a coffin. Every time she closed her eyes she saw Tom, the way the bones of his face weren't quite right any more, the smear of blood on his scalp, the glassy look in his eyes. The birds would've returned to him after she left and she felt guilty about that. But she had to go.

She heard an electronic ping she didn't recognise coming from somewhere. She sat up and lifted her jeans from the floor. Fished her phone out the pocket and pressed the button. Nothing. She looked around the room for a few seconds then remembered. Tom's cheap Nokia, the one he only ever used for her. She had lifted it from the Inch and brought it home. While Hal was cooking earlier she brought it upstairs and stashed it in the drawer of her bedside table.

She opened the drawer, picked it up and swiped. A text message from an unknown number:

I know you were there.

She dropped the phone on the bed and her hand shot to her temple. She felt dizzy. What the hell? She stared at the phone lying on the covers then glanced out of the window, dark except for a lighthouse blip in the distance.

She turned back to the phone, picked it up, gripping it tight in her fist, stared at the words until the screen went dark. She brought it back to life and sent a reply.

Who is this?

She pressed send and waited. Someone had Tom's number and

knew that she had his phone. They must've seen her take it from the island. So they were there. It must be the murderer, unless they were bluffing. Maybe it was someone who knew she'd been sleeping with him, someone putting stuff together, fishing for information.

No answer.

She tried to call but there was no caller ID and the phone just bleeped out. She tried again, same result. Then she texted:

How do you have this number?

She stared at the screen, the green of it the only light in the darkness. She checked back through the phone's history, texts and calls, but the only other interactions had been with her own phone.

Then she heard a noise coming from downstairs. A clattering about in the hall, the clomping of feet. She swallowed hard and took a long, slow breath. More thumping around, indistinct, then finally a familiar sound, girlish giggles and comedy shushing, two voices. Iona was back from her shift, and not alone. Again.

There was the sound of a glass smashing, mumbled swearing, a thud against a wall. She was probably fine down there, whoever she was with. But ... Surtsey arched out of bed, still holding Tom's phone. The touch of her toes on the floor made her feel connected, like she was an ancient tree. Shit, that grass was stronger than Halima's usual stuff. She checked the phone screen again, to make sure she hadn't hallucinated it. The message and her reply were still there. She threw on her old green hoodie, put the phone in the pouch pocket and headed downstairs, peeling her feet from the floor then replacing them like a badly programmed robot.

Iona was in the kitchen staring at bits of wine glass on the floor. She wore a tight Ramones T-shirt and black shorts, her legs long and tanned, that snake tattoo up her left thigh. Her dyed-red hair was in a mess across her face. Behind her was a guy, big and dumb-looking, sleeve tattoos and a black shirt, jeans hanging off his arse.

Iona looked up and beamed a smile.

'Sis,' she said. 'Fuck.'

She waved at the floor of glass between them.

'Fucking broke.'

She put a hand out to steady herself. Surtsey looked at the clock on the microwave, 3:17am. If she'd finished at The Espy at one, that meant only two hours of drinking. How could she be this wasted? Unless she started earlier.

The dumb guy nodded. 'Hey.'

'Hey,' Surtsey said.

Iona seemed to notice him for the first time. 'Sur, this is Jez. From Sydney.'

'Sur,' Jez said, 'cool name.'

Surtsey scoped the guy with a slow gaze while she stroked the phone in her pocket. She looked at Iona and widened her eyes. 'Really?'

Iona didn't notice or ignored it. 'Join us for a snifter, sis.' She looked around and spotted a half-full wine bottle on the worktop. She stotted over to it, glass crunching under her Doc boots.

'I'm all right,' Surtsey said.

Something occurred to Iona. 'Hey, is the H-bomb still up? Wouldn't mind a wee toke.'

'She's asleep.'

Iona made exaggerated head movements, looking around. 'Maybe there's some shit around here somewhere.'

Jez stood there filling up space, smiling like a chimp.

Surtsey needed to get out of there.

'See you in the morning,' she said, leaving the kitchen. She walked into the living room, pocketed Halima's pipe and grass then went to the front door. She pushed her feet into flowery wellies, pulled on her Parka and left the house.

It was already the next day outside. The sky light behind Berwick Law, orange tracers into blue, high wisps of cloud glowing in the pre-dawn. Oil tankers with their lights on in the mouth of the firth, the street lights across in Fife. And the Inch, a dark presence against the violet sky to the west, an absence of light like a miniature black hole in the sea. Surtsey stared at it for a long time, thinking about the message.

She looked up and down the prom, but there was no one in sight. Eventually she climbed over the wall and jumped down to the beach. She kicked the wellies off, wanted to feel connected to the sand. Scrunched her toes into it then walked towards the sea, the tide well out, a hundred yards of squelching underfoot until the soft whisper of the waves. She stepped in up to her calves, the bottoms of her pyjamas soaked. She held her breath against the cold, felt her heart quicken, involuntary reactions, no thought required.

She pulled the pipe and grass out, packed the bowl and lit it. Sucked, kept it in her lungs, imagined she was made of magma. She exhaled, tried to picture her spirit leaving her body along with the smoke, up into the atmosphere, circling the earth with the air currents forever.

She was really wasted.

Someone knew, that's all she could figure out. Someone was there, had seen her, and knew. But who? How?

She stared east. The sun would rise in an hour. She would have to get up, go to the office and pretend everything was OK. She closed her eyes and realised she couldn't feel the coldness of the water any more. You could get used to anything, it seemed.

6

Surtsey stood outside the hospice and tried to clear her head. The small windows of the building's observation tower were blazing in the sunshine, making her squint. She'd slept for four hours, crashing when the grass buzz wore off. She woke in a fug, then remembered. Ran to the toilet and puked in the sink, tasting grass and red wine. She spent a few minutes staring in the mirror, straightening her shit out, then got dressed and tried to anchor herself to the day.

She had her back to the sea now as if she wasn't speaking to it for what it had subjected her to. She took Tom's phone out of her pocket and checked it. Nothing. She'd found an old charger cable in a drawer last night, charged it up overnight. She shook her head at the phone now, lifted the screen to her forehead, felt its coolness, then put it back in her pocket.

She thought of Alice waking up this morning, frantic that her husband wasn't home, that he hadn't been in touch.

Her neck was stiff and heavy, and she cricked it as she opened the gate.

St Columba's was one of four old, sprawling buildings on the prom, nestled between the Joppa terraces at the east end and the more modest buildings further west. In a previous life it had been a kids' nursery, so had swapped one regime of nappy changing and cleaning up sick for another. Next to it were two privately owned Gothic homes, all steep turrets and high walled gardens, then at the far end was the scuffed up Dalriada pub, wooden pirate with broken cutlass standing outside and sit-in folk sessions most nights. Together, the four houses were like a huddle of dishevelled elderly ladies gazing out to sea.

The hospice building was unique with its square observation tower jutting from the crooks and crevices. Surtsey didn't know if it ever got used. Most of the inmates, as Louise called them, couldn't get up the spiral staircase, Louise herself once abandoning an expedition when she couldn't lift her drip-bag frame past the second step. You would get a great view from up there, East Lothian, Fife, the teardrop of the Inch between.

Surtsey sighed and pushed the front door open.

Effie on reception met her with a smile. New folk coming through the door got the professional face, but after you visited a while Effie broke the mask and there was kindness in her eyes. She was well under five feet tall, with a thin face and large-framed glasses on a string of purple beads around her neck. Her long grey hair was always in some intricate arrangement, today it was plaits looped over her head like a pretzel, giving her the appearance of a Ukrainian matriarch.

Surtsey touched a finger against the reception desk. 'Hi, Effie, how's she been?'

Effie nodded with her mouth turned down. 'OK.' Which meant anything but.

'Did she sleep?'

'Not much. A bit like yourself, looking at you.'

Surtsey lifted her finger from the oak up to her temple, where it fluttered. 'I'm fine.'

Effie smiled. 'Candle at both ends, eh?'

'Not exactly.' Surtsey looked along the corridor to the left. 'Where is she?'

'Rec room,' Effie said, nodding. 'Away in.'

Surtsey's stomach was tight as she walked. She came to see Mum every day, twice if possible, but it was never easy, she had to steel herself each time. She understood why Iona stayed away, she would herself if she could.

The rec room was quiet, two old dears bowed over knitting in the far corner. One of the disadvantages of dying from cancer in her forties was that everyone else in the place was twice Louise's age. Louise sat at one of the large bay windows looking out to sea, thin blanket over her knees.

This wasn't her mother, but it was. On the one hand Surtsey didn't want this wasted, six-stone shell of a woman to be the mum she remembered after she was gone. She wanted to picture the vibrant woman slipping off her shoes in the sand and dancing with Surtsey and her sister, kicking up her dress as she ran round the bases at rounders, cigarette hanging from her mouth.

But then she didn't want to deny dignity to this woman in front of her either. This really was her mother, this was every molecule, every pore, every inch the same woman who gave birth to her after thirty-six long hours, who raised her and her sister alone, who fed and clothed them and took them out of school on exotic working holidays at a moment's notice, to earthquake zones and volcanoes in the middle of jungles, high on desert plateaus, adrift on arctic seas.

And here she was with half her stomach and bowel hacked away by surgery, what remained riddled with aggressive carcinoma. Ironic that someone who smoked all her life ended up getting stomach not lung cancer, but there you go.

'Hey, Mum.'

Surtsey touched her mum's shoulder and kissed the top of her head, the short hair rough against her lips. Louise had shaved her head a while back when chemo was an option, then never went bald. One of cancer's wee jokes. But she kept it short anyway, it was easier. When you needed a nurse to cut your food and wipe your arse, not having to keep your hair shiny was one less piece of crap to worry about.

Louise turned and smiled, held out a hand. Surtsey took it and sat down. Her mum's skin felt like nylon, artificial somehow. She smelt bitter, acrid. Could you smell of cancer? Weren't there dogs that detected early signs of it in humans?

'How are you?' Surtsey said.

'I'm dying.'

'Nice day for it.'

This was a running joke. Louise threw out the line, Surtsey batted it straight back, although it was getting less funny every day, and Surtsey wished they hadn't started it.

Louise's breath was laboured, a wheeze deep in her chest. She had a handkerchief in her other hand, brought it up and dabbed at her mouth, dribbled into it. Surtsey looked away for a moment.

'Anything happening in the world?' Louise said.

Surtsey examined her. Forty-five years old and reduced to clock watching, waiting to die. She was so physically diminished it was as if she might shrink to death. Surtsey tried to picture the vibrant presence of her mother in her childhood, but the truth was this image in front of her was replacing that one.

'Not really,' she said.

Louise coughed, dabbed at her lips. 'Up to much last night?'

Of course, Surtsey had skipped the after-work visit to sneak around with Tom. Christ. The last time Surtsey saw her mum, Tom was alive. That seemed impossible. It already felt like he'd always been dead, lying out there waiting to be found. Surtsey took her hand from Louise's and rubbed at her own jaw.

'Out with Brendan.'

Louise tried to smile. 'How are things between you two?'

'OK.'

'Wow, sounds like true love.'

'It's good, things are good.'

Louise coughed but was too slow in getting the handkerchief to her mouth, green spit down her T-shirt. She dabbed at it until Surtsey pulled a tissue from her pocket and wiped, feeling the knobbly breastbone beneath.

Louise tried to push Surtsey's hand away. 'I don't need help.'

'Yes, you do, that's why you're in here.'

'I don't need help from you, is what I meant.'

'I'm your daughter.'

'Exactly.'

Surtsey folded the damp tissue away and stuffed it in her pocket. Louise was gazing out the window, the shoulder of the Inch to her left, Inchkeith behind. Surtsey tried to imagine what the view was like thirty years ago before the Inch was born. The island had always been in her life, a permanent presence, but nothing was permanent, just think of the Cockenzie chimneys, now gone. Or Louise. Or Tom.

'How's your sister?' Louise said.

Surtsey took a breath. 'You would know how she was if she ever bothered to visit.'

'Don't, Sur.' Louise shook her head. 'She's busy.'

'Don't make excuses for her.'

'It's hard for her.'

'And it's easy for me?' Surtsey hated how she sounded, small and bitter.

Louise turned to meet Surtsey's gaze. 'You're strong.'

'I don't feel strong.'

Louise coughed some more, held the hankie to her mouth, her body shuddering as if she might shake apart.

Surtsey put a hand on her mum's back, didn't move it, just left it there, connected.

'Are you OK, Louise?'

A familiar voice behind them.

Surtsey turned to see Donna in her pastel scrubs. Tall and broad, strong cheekbones and nose, dark brown hair tied in a loose pony-tail. One of the million coincidences that happened in a small place like Portobello, someone from the year below you at school winds up nursing your dying mother.

'Fine,' Louise said, still spluttering.

'Hey, Donna,' Surtsey said.

Donna smiled. 'Hi.'

Surtsey hadn't really been friends with Donna at school, she was only vaguely aware of her presence in the year below, saw her in corridors, playgrounds or the lunchtime queue at the sandwich place, then later nestled in a different corner of the Dalriada with her own friends. But since Louise came to St Columba's they'd got to know each other better, brought together in the worst circumstances.

'Maybe I need to lie down,' Louise said.

'Let me get your wheelchair,' Surtsey said.

'Donna can do it,' Louise said, 'it's her job.'

Surtsey watched as Donna positioned the chair, wrapped her arms around Louise and lifted her in. She turned Louise from the view and began pushing her away.

'I'll see you tonight, Mum,' Surtsey said.

Louise tried to smile, her head drooping with the effort. 'Love you, Sur.'

'Love you.'

As they passed Surtsey she lifted an eyebrow to Donna, who shook her head. Surtsey always tried to get a word with Donna about her mum when she visited, something more than the official record of her deterioration. Donna pushed Louise past then turned back to Surtsey. She tapped her watch and held up five fingers. Surtsey nodded.

7

They grabbed lattes from the green Citroen van at the bottom of Bell-field Street then sat on the wall outside the old swimming baths.

Surtsey nodded at Donna's cup. 'Should you be having that after the graveyard shift?'

'I'll be fine,' Donna said, taking a sip. 'I like working nights, actually. It doesn't suit everyone, but it gives me time to think.'

Donna was taller than Surtsey and a bit curvier. She was pretty in a homely way, and seemed wiser than other folk their age. Maybe it was perspective from working with the terminally ill. Sitting here in the morning sunlight, their legs dangling over the sand, Surtsey felt like she was a big sister, someone to look out for her at a time when Surtsey had to look after everyone else.

'How's Mum doing?' Surtsey said.

Donna looked at her. 'Not great.'

Surtsey turned away, the look in Donna's eyes too much.

'I just want her to be comfortable,' Surtsey said.

'She is, trust me.'

Surtsey shook her head. 'I feel so guilty, I should be looking after her.'

She felt Donna's hand on hers.

'Louise was right back there, I get paid to look after her,' Donna said. 'She's in the best hands, even if I say so myself.'

Surtsey felt tears coming, tried to blink them away. She slipped her hand away from Donna's and took a sip of coffee. She was deliberately not looking west to the Inch, her face turned upwards to the sun in the other direction.

She knew Donna was studying her, could feel her gaze without looking.

'You don't look like you had a very good night,' Donna said.

'No.'

'Out on the town?'

'Hardly.' Surtsey didn't say anything else.

'It's none of my business,' Donna said.

Surtsey was silent for a long time. 'I don't know what I'm doing.'

The hash was still burning through her synapses.

More silence for a while. A cormorant scudded along the surface of the water then landed on a groyne and faced the sun with its wings open like a meditating Buddhist.

'How's your love life?' Surtsey said eventually.

Donna laughed. 'What love life?'

'There must be guys interested, you're a good-looking girl.'

'Who works odd shifts and deals with the dying.' Donna looked mortified for a moment. 'Sorry, I didn't mean...'

'It's OK.' Surtsey smiled at her. 'So you don't get a chance to get kinky with your nurse's uniform?'

Donna touched the material of her scrubs and laughed warmly. 'You've seen my uniform, right?'

Joggers and cyclists throbbed up and down the prom, parents taking their kids to Towerbank along the road, their red uniforms little flashes of future promise. Surtsey watched them and felt like an imposter. She felt like she'd been living someone else's life since last night. How could she square that with sitting here drinking latte and chatting on a beautiful summer morning, the shush of waves and the noise of kids, dogs snuffling around their feet and gulls pecking at the bins along the way, old folk doddering down the steps from the baths.

'There's something I have to tell you,' Donna said. 'About Louise.'

'Let me guess, she's going to die.'

'Surtsey.'

'Sorry.'

Donna hesitated, her thumb flicking at the polystyrene lid of her coffee. 'She asked about pain medication.'

'She's on a lot of morphine already, right?'

'I don't mean that,' Donna said. 'I mean additional medication.'

'So what?'

'Large amounts of it.'

It took Surtsey a second. 'Oh. Shit.'

'Sorry.'

Surtsey looked out to sea. Flat and shimmering this morning, untroubled.

'You didn't give her any?'

'God, no,' Donna said. 'Technically I'm supposed to report it to my supervisor.'

'But you didn't?'

'No.'

'Thanks.'

'Maybe you could have a word with her?'

Surtsey sighed. 'Christ.' She saw tears in Donna's eyes. 'Hey, don't be stupid.'

'I feel so bad having to tell you,' Donna said, 'but I thought you should know.'

Surtsey touched Donna's wrist, a leather friendship bracelet there. 'You did the right thing.'

Silence for a moment, Surtsey's hand still on Donna's bracelet. She thought about her mum, was she really trying to get enough pills together to end it herself? How the hell was she supposed to bring something like that up in casual conversation? And why hadn't she spoken to Surtsey about it first?

'You're a good daughter,' Donna said eventually.

'I'm not so sure.'

'You are.'

'Yeah, well.' Surtsey noticed the time on her watch. 'Shit. I really better get over to KB.'

She didn't move for a moment, just breathed, then swivelled and hopped off the wall.

'No rest for the wicked,' Donna said.

'Something like that.'

8

All the way on the 42 bus Surtsey tried to get her heart to beat like normal. She breathed carefully as they trundled past Peffermill and Cameron Toll, in through the nose, out through the mouth. Or was it meant to be the other way round?

She jumped off at the bottom of Mayfield and crossed West Mains Road. The Grant Institute was a brown 1930s block on the edge of campus facing over the road, home to geology and geophysics, including her, Halima, Brendan and the rest. Edinburgh Uni enticed students to come with the promise of vibrant student life up in George Square, bars, cafes and clubs, being in the thick of the festival in summer. Then after first year undergrad they shoved you out here with all the other science nerds, surrounded by posh houses and fields, half an hour on the bus from town.

She went through the front door and up the stairs to their open-plan department office. Somehow it always managed to be gloomy in here even on sunny days.

The room was half full, six folk checking social media or reading news on screens, one or two actually doing some writing or fiddling with data analysis. Halima and Brendan both smiled at her as she went to the kettle, but she didn't stop. She spooned instant coffee into her mug and waited for the kettle to boil. She stared at Tom's empty office at the end of the room. The door was open, but then the door was always open. That was one of the good things about Tom as a boss, there was no sense of superiority, no us-and-them.

Surtsey felt dizzy. Her eyes defocused then came back as the kettle switched off. She poured, splashing water onto the table.

'Got some gossip.'

The voice made her twitch and she spilled more water, splats of it on the floor between her feet.

It was Halima. 'Shit, babes, watch yourself, you nearly boiled your shoes there.'

Surtsey put the kettle down and stirred her coffee.

Halima grinned. 'Apparently Tom's gone missing.'

'What?'

'No one has seen our beloved professor since yesterday.' Halima was mugging like a detective.

Surtsey looked at her watch and shook her head.

'He'll just be coming in late.'

Halima wagged a finger in the air. 'His wife was here first thing this morning asking if anyone had seen him.'

'Alice was here?' Surtsey looked round.

'Where were you, by the way?' Halima said. 'I thought maybe you'd pulled a sickie. That new grass is crazy.'

'I went to see Mum.'

Halima's goofball face faded. 'Of course, sorry.'

Surtsey picked up her coffee but it was too hot to drink so she put it down again. 'What did Alice say?'

'She was frantic. He told her he was working late yesterday, that old line, but then he didn't come home. She tried his phone, nothing. Still nothing this morning.'

'Has she called the police?'

'They can't waste manpower on a search,' Halima said. 'No crime against going missing, they said.'

'Really?'

Halima's goon face was back. 'He's going to be in some heavy shit when he turns up.'

'You don't think he's in trouble?'

'What sort of trouble?'

Surtsey just wanted this to end. 'Car accident? Heart attack?'

'Someone would've found him, contacted the police. Anyway, Alice said she already phoned round the hospitals. Nothing. The plot thickens.'

'Don't, Hal, he could be in real trouble.'

'Ach, he's fine. He'll be on a bender or shagging some daft undergrad. Minor midlife crisis. He'll turn up sheepish, get a bollocking, then be welcomed back into the fold.'

Surtsey went to pick up her coffee again, but her finger slipped on the handle and liquid sloshed on to the floor.

Halima stepped back and narrowed her eyes. 'You OK? That was some strong shit last night.'

'I'm fine.'

'Iona clattering about with that guy didn't help. Some girl.'

'Yeah.' Surtsey glanced at Tom's office, then at her own desk. 'I'd better get on.'

'Still on for lunch, yeah?'

Surtsey nodded, went to her desk and logged in. First thing she did was a Google news search for 'the Inch' and 'Tom Lawrie'. Nothing much, just some old puff pieces from months ago, when they got that research grant. A picture of Tom on the *Evening Standard* website alongside one of the iconic pictures of the Inch, bloody lava pouring along the crevice between volcanic vent and flat plain, white steam billowing in a column where the lava fizzled in contact with the sea. She had the same picture on a postcard next to her computer monitor. Those early aerial shots of the island were inspiration to everyone who worked here, the idea of newly created land emerging from the ocean depths. It was beautiful, like anyone could get a new start in life given the right circumstances.

Surtsey clicked the story away, brought up the department homepage. She went into her browser history and deleted this morning's search.

'Was Halima telling you about Tom?'

Brendan was next to her desk, running his finger along the edge of the wood. She had a pang in her heart, a rush of remembering why she'd fallen for him in the first place, the dark curly hair and freckles, the green eyes, bags of energy. Why had she bothered looking elsewhere? She should've spoken to him already, it must've looked weird not to when she came in, but she couldn't face him just now.

'Yeah,' she said.

'Strange, eh?' That soft Dublin sliver of voice.

'I'm sure he'll turn up.'

Brendan rubbed at his knuckles.

'Up to much last night?'

Surtsey stared at her computer screen. The uni logo, the panorama of Edinburgh's skyline, the castle along to Salisbury Crags, the edge of the Inch poking out behind the rump of Arthur's Seat. The picture was taken from the observatory at Blackford Hill along the road, which meant if she could get up high enough, she could see the Inch from here. Edinburgh was such a small place.

'Night in with Hal,' she said.

Brendan nodded, puppy eyes. 'Fancy doing something tonight?'

Surtsey touched her temple. 'I'm feeling a bit shit at the moment, let me think about it.'

'Sure.'

She could sense his disappointment and felt guilty.

Brendan shuffled his feet. 'How about lunch?'

She nodded across the office. 'Hal has stuff going on, man problems. I said I'd help her talk it out. Sorry.'

Brendan hovered for a moment. 'Everything's OK, yeah?'

Surtsey put on a smile. 'Fine, just a bit spaced. And Mum's worse.'

'Sorry.'

She was ashamed to use Louise like that but it worked. Brendan frowned and moved away from her desk.

'OK, take it easy,' he said, shoulders slumped.

Surtsey scrolled down on the screen, moved the cursor over the link to Tom's department page, but didn't click.

*

She picked at a stale panini in the KB Café and gazed at the concrete and metal clutter out the window as Halima prattled on, something about Iona that Surtsey probably should be listening to. She looked around, couldn't see Brendan anywhere. Maybe he went to the union for a burger. She felt sick at the thought of eating, stared at her tuna melt in disgust.

'Anyway, we'd better get our shit together,' Halima said, standing up and lifting her empty plate.

'What for?'

'Sample trip,' Halima said. 'Not like you to forget.'

Oh shit. Fucking shit. They were due to collect rock samples from the Inch and Surtsey had blanked it from her mind. She couldn't, she just couldn't.

'I can't go,' she said.

'Don't be stupid, you love it on that rock, come on.'

Surtsey shook her head. 'I forgot, I have something on.'

'No you don't, what's up?'

Surtsey thought for a moment. 'I don't feel well.'

Halima shook her head. 'You're just hungover, a bit of sea air will sort you out. The minibus is going in ten minutes.'

'Seriously, Hal, I can't.'

Halima frowned. 'You're coming, missus, if I have to drag you myself.'

'I'm not.'

'Look.' Halima's voice was serious all of a sudden. 'I need your help out there. You know Rachel has been riding me for better data. I need as many samples as I can get and this is the last scheduled trip for a fortnight. I can't wait that long. And you're the best there is with a rock hammer.'

Surtsey sighed and got up, leaving her sandwich where it was. It would look worse if she didn't go, and maybe this was what she deserved. It had been coming ever since she left the Inch, left him, last night.

9

Her lifejacket was too tight under the arms, the fabric biting her skin. The spray in her face reminded her of last night, and she turned to look back at Portobello beach as it receded. The symmetry of the groynes breaking up the sand, the scattered blocks of tenements and houses, the Beach House, the Espy, then the amusements and an ice cream stand. All of it busy, people getting on with their lives, a handful of tourists taking selfies with the view. She'd lived her whole life on this piece of coast but she'd never felt more disconnected from it than right now.

The sea was choppy today, the colour of sludge, as they powered to the island. She stared at the wash spreading back to shore, disappearing amongst the expanse of water. They were skimming the surface of this territory, interlopers, only passing time until the water decided to take everything back.

This boat was much bigger than her one, a twelve-seat rigid hull with decent horsepower. It had the Edinburgh Uni logo on the prow, and they kept it at the Portobello Yacht Club lock-up next to the Beach House. Rachel – Dr Worthington – was steering, swinging the rudder and turning the prow to point at the Inch. There were six PhDs in the boat, Surtsey, Halima and Brendan, along with three first years for whom this was an exciting new adventure.

Surtsey took in gulps of air and turned to look at the Inch. It was much more dramatic than the other islands in the Forth which were worn by millions of years of weather and erosion, covered in thick grass and derelict war defences. In comparison the black cliffs on the eastern side of the Inch were monolithic and ominous, and the spreads of volcanic rock and lava were a moonscape. The peaks were hollowed out cones, the promise of smoke and flames lingering, although they hadn't erupted in five years. In geological time, of course, the Inch wasn't even the blink of an eye, not even a tick on the clock. Which was one of the reasons scientists came here, to study how new land adapted after being born and to find out how life colonised the space, birds, seaborne plants and the rest.

She was relieved that the roar of the engine along with the wind and spray made it impossible to speak, she couldn't handle conversation. Brendan caught her eye, a look that said he was worried, and Halima too, maybe thinking Surtsey might puke over the side because of last night.

Surtsey held on to the side of the boat as it bumped over waves. Rachel angled them towards the northern point of the teardrop, the short jetty. They slowed on approach, turned alongside the jetty and cut the engine.

Surtsey looked at the beach where her footprints had been, wiped away by the last high tide. She wondered about the nearby cove. Did she leave any trace above the tide line? She tried to think. All she could picture was the matted hair at the top of Tom's skull, the spread of black on the sand, the sound of birds squabbling.

Halima tied up the boat and they trooped off carrying sample kits and tools in branded backpacks. They headed southeast away from the cove to the site next to the cliffs. The idea was to examine different marked-out areas, compare soil types, rock formations, the effects of erosion already, and also any plant or animal life. The last wasn't in their remit but they notified the biology department about it.

They spread out and began working. The sun was high and Surtsey built up a sweat in T-shirt and jeans as she scraped at the soil, shovelling samples into ziplock bags, marking coordinates, date and time, all the mundane stuff of science that never made it onto TV shows. Hundreds of days like today, students doing grunt work so that professors could present findings and come to conclusions, be awarded prizes and appear at conferences and dinners. Not that Tom would see any more of that.

It came as a strange relief when she heard the screams. Finally it was happening, something to react to.

They were on a break, two hours after arriving. Juice bottles and chocolate, the odd piece of fruit.

Surtsey had her face to the sun, the burn on her skin. She kept her eyes closed for a moment when the screaming started, tried to guess who it was. Rachel? Kezia?

She opened her eyes and squinted, tried to focus. Kezia and Brendan were the only ones not here, so it must be her. Were those two friends now? Was Brendan moving on to someone younger and happier?

Halima and Rachel stood, shielding their eyes as they looked west over the edge of the hill. Watching, waiting. Alex and Sean began walking up the rise towards the noise.

The screaming stopped and was replaced by shouts, Brendan's voice.

Surtsey got up as Brendan appeared on the horizon, waving for them to come. Alex and Sean hurried towards him as Kezia appeared behind.

Halima threw Surtsey a look. 'What the hell?'

They all went, Surtsey at the back, tethered to them by an invisible rope.

Brendan was already explaining something to the boys, holding Kezia's shoulder as she buried her face in her hands. Rachel was with them now, then Halima, Surtsey yards behind. Brendan repeated himself for Rachel then again for Halima. Surtsey watched the rest of them, how they reacted, searching for clues about how to behave. Shock, horror, disbelief. She tried them on, see how they felt.

'It's Tom,' Brendan said. 'We found his body. He's dead.'

Shock. Horror. Disbelief.

Surtsey really felt them, let her face feel them.

'Tell us exactly what happened,' Rachel said. She suddenly seemed much older than the rest of them, someone in charge.

Brendan was out of breath. He swapped a glance with Kezia whose face crumpled in tears.

'We went for a walk,' Brendan said. 'Back to the jetty then round to the next cove. There was something on the beach, the gulls were on it. I thought it was a dead seal at first but we got closer and I spotted shoes. Christ.'

Kezia sniffled, not looking up.

'We went to look,' Brendan said. 'It's Tom.'

Rachel had her authority face on. 'You're sure?'

Brendan nodded.

'He's dead?'

'Yeah.'

'Did you check his pulse?'

Brendan shook his head. 'He's been there a while. He had no eyes. His eyes are gone. Fucking birds.'

Kezia let out a burst of tears and snot.

Halima put a hand to her mouth.

'Jesus Christ,' Rachel said.

Surtsey pictured Tom in bed with her, gazing at her body, kindness in his eyes. Maybe more, maybe love. Who knew what someone else was ever thinking?

'I'll call the police,' Rachel said, getting her phone out. She turned to Brendan. 'Can you show me?'

'I suppose.'

'Come on.' Rachel took him by the arm, touching her phone screen as she went.

The only sound was Kezia sniffing.

'I can't get my head round it,' Halima said.

Alex and Sean swore under their breaths.

'This is going to kill Alice,' Halima said.

'Yeah,' Surtsey said.

'What was he doing out here?' Halima said.

Surtsey shook her head. 'The police will sort it out.'

Halima looked around at the four of them. She pulled the hash pipe and grass out of her pocket. 'I could use a smoke. Anyone else?'

Alex and Sean frowned and shook their heads.

Kezia looked disgusted. 'The police will be here soon.'

Halima turned to Surtsey. 'Sur?'

Surtsey stared at her. 'Spark it up.'

It took ninety minutes for the police to show up and the wait was excruciating. What do you do in that vacuum? They couldn't go back to work, out of the question. They didn't want to be near the body, too horrifying. Surtsey and Halima had a quick smoke before Rachel came back with Brendan. Surtsey was stoned and scared she might start giggling at the absurdity of it all, stuck on an island in the middle of nowhere with a dead body. Rachel decided they should pack up and wait at the jetty. More awkward silence there, Kezia still blubbing away like she personally owned the shock. Fuck that, thought Surtsey, I was close to him, not you. I should have first dibs on the grief here.

Brendan tried to reassure her, seeing it as his boyfriend duty, but she just shrugged, gave him a hug then wandered off to be alone on the beach. She had to be away from it all, couldn't stand the silence of the others. She wanted to scream, pick up clumps of wet sand and hurl them into the sea, smash rocks with her hammer, run up the side of the hill and throw herself into the crater, plummet into the searing magma oceans at the earth's core, cause a chain reaction that would detonate the planet from the inside, throw pieces of the world into the universe where they could never be reassembled.

She sat on the sand and listened to the waves.

Eventually she heard an engine and saw the police markings on the black boat as it thrust round the coast towards the jetty. She watched as everyone else got up to meet them. She took juddering breaths, trying to calm her heart, then stood up, wiped the sand from her hands and walked to the jetty.

By the time she got there most of the police were out of the boat. Two tall officers in uniform with black lifejackets, and two women and a man in plain clothes carrying boxes and backpacks of equipment.

They were presumably forensics. The last one out of the boat was an older guy with a beer gut who needed a hand from one of the younger officers to keep his balance as the boat bobbed. He had a red face and patchy beard, the skin of a heavy drinker. He didn't look comfortable in the sunshine, sweat patches on his shirt.

'I'm DCI Jason Yates,' he said, once everyone had gathered round. 'We got a call from Rachel Worthington?'

'That's me.'

'OK, love, how about you get me up to speed.'

Rachel bristled at 'love' but didn't say anything. Surtsey caught Halima's eye roll and suppressed a smile. It amazed her that pricks like this still existed in the modern world, but she came across them all the time.

Rachel went over everything, introduced Brendan and Kezia, pointed in the direction of Tom's body, then the opposite direction where they'd been working.

Yates frowned. 'And the rest of you haven't been over there?'

Shaking heads.

Yates pointed at Rachel, Brendan and Kezia. 'You three show the body to me and the boffins. The rest of you stay here and give statements to my officers.'

Boffins, what an arsehole.

Kezia let out a whimper but went along with the others, leaving the four of them with the two uniforms, a man and a woman about the same age as Surtsey. She wondered what made people sign up for the police force, did they really think they could make a difference? Maybe it was just the salary and pension. She couldn't imagine having that moral certainty, the presumption of superiority over another person. Upholding the law was such a weird phrase. Did anything else get upheld? Surtsey wondered how stoned she was.

She got the male officer to talk to. His name badge said 'Ferris' which made Surtsey think of that 80s movie her mum loved. She glanced towards land but of course she couldn't see Joppa from here, just the spread of Cockenzie and the Pans.

The interview with Officer Ferris took three minutes, the cop leaning in to hear her better, despite the fact he was recording the conversation with a handheld Sony device. Surtsey tried not to sound stoned. She kept her voice level but that just made it sound like a robotic monotone in her ears. She gave her details and explained she hadn't seen the body.

'And when did you last see Mr Lawrie?' Ferris said.

Surtsey stood for a moment. She heard an insect buzzing some-where, wondered briefly about pollination, the spread of life.

'Yesterday,' she said. 'At the department, same as everyone else.'

She expected him to ask what she was up to last night. A tremor in her chest as she thought about what she'd told others, whether it had even been consistent. But he didn't ask. She wasn't a suspect, no one here was; they were friends and colleagues. Just answer the questions you're asked, Surtsey.

'OK, thanks,' Ferris said.

He switched the recorder off and looked around at the black sand, the grey rock, the bubbles and crenulations of the lava.

'Some place, this,' he said.

'Yeah.'

Surtsey was so used to the Inch that she worried she would take it for granted. But she never did. It was remarkable, a baby island, a part of the world that hadn't existed twenty-five years ago.

'Surtsey's an interesting name,' Ferris said.

She got asked about it all the time.

'I'm named after an Icelandic island,' she said. 'A volcanic island, like this one, that erupted in the 60s. My mum says it's her favourite place in the world. She's a volcanologist, like me. Actually, I was born the day this place erupted.'

'But she didn't want to call you Inch.'

Surtsey laughed despite herself. 'I suppose not.'

'When you think about it, it's not using much imagination, calling it the Inch.'

Surtsey touched her hair and smiled. 'It's not.'

Was she really flirting with a cop as her dead lover lay on the beach, eyes pecked out by gulls?

'So you like all this,' Ferris said, waving his hand. 'Rocks and stuff.'

Surtsey laughed again. 'Yeah, I like rocks and stuff.'

He laughed with her and she smiled. It was pathetic but she liked it. It felt normal, chatting as if they were in a café or pub, as if there wasn't something grotesque lying just out of sight.

There was the scrunch of feet on gravel. DCI Yates appeared puffing up the slope, Rachel, Kezia and Brendan behind.

Ferris and the female cop straightened up. What was it like having to kowtow to authority all the time, Surtsey thought.

'You got their statements?' Yates asked.

'Yes, sir,' the female cop said. Surtsey noticed that Ferris had deferred to her, let her speak for them both. Not a big deal in the scheme of things, but a noticeable gesture.

'OK, you can all go,' Yates said. 'We'll be in touch with you individually if we need anything else. The island is off limits until I say so.'

He was the kind of man used to authority, it made him feel important.

Ferris raised his eyebrows at Surtsey, who smiled.

She didn't speak as they all trudged towards the boat, she was just desperate to get off this rock and find a drink.

11

'To Tom.'

The three of them thrust shot glasses together with a clunk, then downed the Jägers. Maybe a single malt was more appropriate but fuck it, Tom wouldn't care. Plus he'd always seemed younger than he was, liked hanging out with students, soaking up their youth and enthusiasm. And screwing them, in Surtsey's case. He would probably have downed a Jägermeister himself, given the chance.

She thought about the text message. Someone knew something, but she couldn't work out how much, or who or how. The message was so vague, no specific detail so maybe they were just fishing. She couldn't fathom how they knew. She and Tom had been cautious about where and when they met, and they had set up his dedicated phone. They occasionally sent emails too, but he set up a new Gmail account for that, not his usual home one, and he never accessed it on his regular phone.

Surtsey looked around. The Espy was dead this time on a Wednesday afternoon. The lunchtime rush was over and the after work crowd hadn't pitched up yet. Her, Brendan and Halima were sitting at the long table by the window which housed the huge fish tank, hundreds of tropical sparkles darting across her eyeline. It was a strange decision by the pub to block the sea view but Surtsey was glad at the moment because it meant the Inch was out of sight. It haunted her, that rock. It had nagged at her ever since she could pull herself up to the living room window ledge and see outside.

'Stone,' she'd apparently shouted, pointing at it, aged two.

Her mum tells the story best, how she explained it was an island, surrounded by water, a long way away. Toddler Surtsey nodded forcefully.

'Stone.'

And it was still her stone, a rock weighing her down. The place that had killed her secret lover. It was weird even saying that word inside her head, lover. Felt like she couldn't do it without sarcastic quotes, without reaching for the sick bag, without it sounding like some 1970s hippy thing. But what else were they? Certainly not boyfriend and girl-friend. Fuckbuddies was too childish.

'So, come on,' Halima said, swigging her large Cabernet.

'What?' Brendan said.

'Let's have the theories,' Halima said.

Surtsey frowned. 'What theories?'

Halima did the eye roll and fake-punched her. 'About what hap-pened to Tom, of course. Our esteemed colleague and boss found with his head caved in.'

'Christ, Hal,' Surtsey said. 'The man's dead.'

Halima shrugged. 'Of course it's awful, but it's a puzzle, right?'

'You can't help wondering,' Brendan said.

Surtsey looked from one to the other. She loved Halima, but wasn't sure she could use the same word for Brendan. He was just a bit of fun, maybe 'fuckbuddy' applied better to him. She knew that she and Tom couldn't have lasted but she realised now she'd invested more in that relationship than the one with Brendan.

'I'm not wondering,' Surtsey said.

'Come on,' Halima said, incredulous. 'What was he doing there? How did he die? Was it an accident? If so, how? During last night's earthquake? If it wasn't an accident then it was murder, so who did it? Did they know him? How did they get on the island? Where's Tom's boat? Is there any trace of this other person?'

She'd been counting on her fingers.

'That's ten unanswered questions right there.'

Her voice had got loud and two middle-aged tourists glanced over. The young mums splitting a bottle of Pinot in the corner while their kids threw Connect Four counters at each other were oblivious.

'I don't know,' Surtsey said.

'Of course you don't,' Halima said. 'I'm looking for speculation here.'

'It was probably an accident,' Brendan said. 'Maybe a rock dislodged during last night's quake and hit him.'

'A rock from where? He was on the beach.'

'Maybe he wasn't knocked out,' Surtsey said. 'Maybe he got concussed and staggered to the beach.'

Halima was wide eyed. 'So where's his boat?'

Brendan shook his head. 'Maybe he didn't moor it properly.'

'That's not like him,' Surtsey said. She was surprised to find herself contributing to this.

'True,' Halima said.

'Hey, how are my favourite nerds?'

It was Iona standing over the table, faded Snoopy T-shirt with the cleavage cut out of it, tied in a knot at the bottom so it clung to her body. Short black skirt over black leggings. Surtsey noticed Brendan glancing at the curve of her body. She was sexy but she looked exhausted.

'Hey,' Surtsey said.

'I-ball, you'll never guess what happened,' Halima said.

'You got laid for once?' Iona said.

'I'm serious,' Halima said.

Iona looked around the table and put on a frown. 'Judging by the looks on your faces, something sad. Did a report come out that said rocks were really boring?'

Iona had a thing about knowledge. Nihilistic bullshit, nothing was worth doing, the whole world was full of crap, might as well stay dumb and revel in it. Of course it was all a front but you couldn't say that, just had to wait for her to grow up, find something she wanted to do with her life.

'Our boss, Tom, is dead,' Halima said. 'Suspicious circumstances. Brendan found him.'

'Really?' Iona tried to hide her interest.

Brendan nodded. 'Out on the Inch.'

Iona looked over the fish tank out the window. 'Wow, that stupid rock just got interesting. Was the body decomposed?'

'Come on,' Surtsey said.

Iona held her hands out. 'Just asking.'

Brendan shook his head. 'He could only have been there a day, he was in the office yesterday. His eyes were gone, the birds got them.'

'Get any pics?'

'First thing I thought of when I found him,' Brendan said, deadpan. 'Snapped a few close ups, put them on Instagram.'

Surtsey smiled and remembered why she liked Brendan.

Iona gave him a look. 'Just asking.' She turned to the others. 'You were there too?'

Surtsey pictured Tom, grains of sand stuck to his face, the angle of his feet. 'We were on the other side of the island.'

'And you didn't go for a peek?'

'We're not all as freaky as you,' Halima said.

'I thought you were supposed to have enquiring scientific minds?' Iona said.

Surtsey had enough. 'Show some respect. This is someone we knew, someone we worked with every day. What the fuck is wrong with you?'

Iona held her hands up like a gun was pointing at her. 'Who rattled your cage?'

Surtsey took a swig of her wine and put the glass down too heavily on the table. She saw Iona giving the other two a look, trying to make them complicit in the idea Surtsey had lost it.

'Have you been to see Mum?' she said.

'Not today.'

'When was the last time you went?'

'I'm busy at work, Sur, you know that.' Iona threw a thumb at the bar. 'I'm just going on shift now.'

Surtsey kept her voice level. 'So what have you been doing all day?'

Iona sighed. 'Don't start.'

'I'm just saying.'

'Don't bother.'

'Unbelievable.'

'You sanctimonious shit.' Iona turned towards the bar.

Surtsey felt her face flush.

'She's your fucking mum too,' she shouted across the bar.

Everyone in the pub paused mid-conversation and stared at her.

Halima and Brendan sipped their drinks and stayed silent as Iona slammed the bar hatch and disappeared into the kitchen through the back.

Surtsey raised her wine but realised the glass was empty.

'Hey, look.' Halima was pointing at the television screen mounted high on the wall in the corner of the pub. BBC News was on, a reporter standing on a familiar beach, the knuckle of the Inch behind her. The sound was down but the ticker tape across the bottom of the screen was already declaring that a body had been found, and naming him as Tom Lawrie. Christ, they didn't hang about.

Surtsey stumbled out of her seat and grabbed the remote from the corner of the bar, punched the volume up. A police spokeswoman was explaining that Tom was an earth science professor who carried out research on the Inch. She used the phrase 'unexplained circumstances' and asked for witnesses. She went on to explain that there was no CCTV on the island, but that someone might have seen a boat embarking or landing sometime the previous evening along the coast. Surtsey thought of her boat in the shed. Could forensics tell anything from that? A trace of black sand on the hull could've been from any time in the past. There was no digital navigation tool to geolocate where she'd been, nothing else to tie her to the scene. As far as she could think.

'Maybe they'll want to interview us,' Halima said.

'They already have,' Surtsey said.

'Not the police, the news people.'

'How would they find us?'

Halima stared at her. 'They're called journalists, you might've heard of them. They look into events, find out stuff, track people down.'

'Yeah, OK.'

'They're got Tom's name so I presume they'll be at the department tomorrow sniffing around.'

Surtsey tried to imagine sitting there tomorrow, looking at Tom's empty office, the picture of Alice and the girls on his desk, the huge map of the Inch on the wall behind, every nook and cranny of the island there to be discovered.

The reporter on the news was now standing in front of a handful of protestors on Portobello beach. There were eight of them, some holding hands and chanting. Two of them held a banner that read: 'Leave New Thule in Peace'. Someone else had his hands aloft, cupped together with a gap in between. It was supposed to represent the teardrop shape of the Inch, but Surtsey thought it looked like a vagina.

'Oh shit,' Halima said. 'I'd forgotten about these guys.'

They were the Children of New Thule, a cult that sprang up once the clouds of steam and ash settled back in 1990 and it was clear that the Inch was here to stay. They were led by some guy called Bastian in square glasses and a neck scarf, an outdoor activist who claimed to have visions that the Inch was spiritual ground never to be desecrated by human feet. They didn't call it the Inch, they called it New Thule, a mythical northern land, somewhere beyond the borders of the known world.

They'd been active in the first few years, protesting against scientific trips to the island, petitioning the public and lobbying government in an attempt to make the Inch protected land. It did end up protected, but by UNESCO as a Site of Special Scientific Significance, not some earthly shrine to a higher power. Bastian and his band of enthusiastic followers took the huff, and spent a couple of years protesting more aggressively, sabotaging boats, vandalising the geophysics department at King's Buildings. It got them noticed in the media but things moved on, most people accepted the Inch was fair game for scientists, and the Children of New Thule slunk back into their hole.

Surtsey hadn't heard from them in ages and had presumed they had disbanded. But now here they were on the national news, Bastian decrying Tom and the department, the entire scientific community, local and national government, anyone who disagreed with his vision. This, he said, was payback from nature, a warning to stay away.

'Surely this dick must be a suspect,' Halima said.

Brendan frowned. 'Then why go on national television with his cronies?'

'Double bluff, it's the last thing anyone would expect.'

Surtsey squinted at the television. Bastion was in his forties, the same generation as her mum. Louise had faced some of the brunt of those early protests, paint splattered across office windows, the department boat filled with fish guts at the lock up. For a while, Bastian had popped up in another guise, a figurehead for the anti-fracking movement. The government had placed a moratorium on fracking across Scotland but hadn't banned it outright. Plenty of companies still ran research and testing voyages in the Forth, hoping one day they'd be able to beat the government and swoop in, start making money. To his credit Bastian had marshalled public support against them, no one wanted toxic sludge and poisoned water supplies on their doorsteps. But the oil companies were still out there collecting data and running feasibility studies.

Then there was the added complication of the Inch. There's no way any company would be allowed to drill for shale anywhere near a UNESCO site. And since Scotland already had earthquakes from the new fault line, it seemed insane to compound that with the possibility of more seismic disturbance from fracking.

With fracking on the backburner, the Inch was clearly back on the agenda for Bastian. He was a charismatic figure, slim, grey beard, sparkling eyes. He was articulate, even if what he said was rubbish. Maybe that's how he'd managed to keep his band of followers for so long. And this was perfect for them, an unfortunate occurrence on the Inch played into their hands, gave them a new lease of life. Or maybe it was more than that, maybe Hal was right, and they had something to do with it. Hiding in plain sight, protesting angrily. Surtsey thought about the text message on her phone.

She dropped the remote control and strode out the pub towards the beach.

12

The dry sand sucked at her trainers as she picked up speed.

'Sur, wait.' Halima's voice, some way behind.

She didn't look back, kept focussed on her target. She noticed over to her right that the BBC outside broadcast van was parked at the bottom of Bellfield Street, across three disabled parking spaces. The reporter from earlier was chatting to her cameraman and a guy wearing headphones and carrying a boom mic. They were clearly off air at the moment, maybe working on what she would say next time they were live.

Ahead of Surtsey the small gang of protestors were chilling too, as if they only put on a show for the camera. The homemade banner was dropped, scuffing the sand, and a young woman with dreadlocks and a long flowing skirt was congratulating Bastian, her body language deferent and submissive.

'Hey,' Surtsey said, loud enough for Bastian and the others to turn around.

Bastian smiled at her like a benevolent teacher, a smile that made Surtsey angry.

She reached them and stopped.

'I saw you on the news,' she said.

Bastian nodded. The calmness of his movements infuriated Surtsey.

'Indeed,' he said.

'How dare you,' Surtsey said.

'I beg your pardon?'

Surtsey waved an arm around, taking in the sea, the beach and the Inch.

'Capitalising on a man's death,' she said.

'I see,' Bastian said, angling his head.

'You should be ashamed.'

'Thule has spoken.' This was the young woman, making that dumb fanny shape with her hands, like a Hindu blessing or something.

Surtsey shook her head. 'A good man has died, and all you can do is spout your spiritual shite. What about his wife and children? His friends?'

Bastian put on a concerned face. 'I take it you were one such friend?'

Surtsey didn't know what to say. Halima and Brendan had caught up with her, she felt a hand on her back, but they didn't speak.

Surtsey thought about Tom's phone, the message.

'Do you recognise me?' she said.

Bastian examined her closely, then shook his head. 'Should I?'

'Did you text me last night?'

Halima touched Surtsey's arm. 'Sur, come on.'

Bastian frowned. 'How could I text you, I don't know you.'

'Thule has spoken,' the hippie woman said again.

'Shut the fuck up,' Halima said. 'What a moron.'

'How do we know you're not involved in this?' Surtsey said to Bastian.

He looked thoughtful. 'We are involved. We are the keepers of New Thule, its protectors. Anything happens on the island, we are involved.'

'I mean, maybe you killed Tom.'

Bastian laughed. 'You clearly don't understand. We are peaceful people.'

'Tom's death seems pretty handy for you,' Surtsey said.

Bastian raised his hands upwards. 'It is divine intervention.'

'You cunt,' Surtsey said. She stepped forward and slapped him in the face, and he made no move to evade her hand, almost leaning in to it.

'Sur, come on,' Brenda said. 'This isn't achieving anything.'

She went to hit him again but Brendan held her arm and pulled her away.

Surtsey stared at Bastian. 'I'm going to get the police on to you.' She looked round the small group, bunch of sheep. 'All of you.'

Bastian smiled.

'Sorry for your loss,' he said.

13

Surtsey tried to compose herself as she stood outside her mum's bedroom at St Columba's, but the wine and adrenaline were making her twitchy. Memories of being drunk and stoned as a teenager came to her, that dreaded moment before going back into the house, having to act sober for a few minutes before you could escape to your bedroom.

She knocked and waited. Important to be respectful, treat Mum like a normal person.

A few seconds of silence.

'Come in.' Wheezy and breathless.

Louise was lying on the bed, a thin crocheted blanket covered in sunflowers spread over her legs. It was a blanket Surtsey's gran had made long ago, a skill that had failed to be passed down the generations. Surtsey wondered if all that vanishing know-how would eventually make them revert back to apes, banging on rocks and scared of fire.

'Hey, Mum, how are you?'

'I'm dying.'

'Mum.'

The lack of energy in Surtsey's voice made Louise frown. 'That's not the punch line.'

Surtsey sighed. 'There isn't a punch line.'

She nodded at the television in the corner of the room, switched off. Might as well get on with it.

'Have you seen the news today, Mum? We found a dead body on the Inch.'

'What?'

Surtsey felt the room wobble. She presumed it was the alcohol, but the look on Louise's face told her it was really happening. Just a small tremor, the kind that happened all the time now in Edinburgh, but still disconcerting. Surtsey spread her feet and tried to balance. She stared at Louise, suspended in the moment, waiting to see if it would escalate into a proper quake or shrug away to nothing. Louise held the sides of her bed. You were supposed to get under furniture or into doorways but usually there was no time for that. A small jolt like this didn't bring down masonry, it only reminded you the world wasn't as stable as you hoped.

'She's restless.' Louise had a habit of talking about the earth as a woman. Being raised in the 70s by hippy parents had planted the Gaia earth mother idea in her head, fuelling her love of geophysics. What was Surtsey's reason? The passing on of the torch, carrying on her mother's life work, investigating the volcanoes and earthquakes that demonstrated the world was alive.

The tremble under their feet stopped, leaving an unsettling calm. Surtsey had been standing with her arms out, palms down, and she moved her hands back to her side.

'It's Tom,' she said.

'What about him?' Louise said.

'The dead person on the Inch. It's Tom Lawrie.'

'My God. What happened?'

Surtsey shook her head. Louise patted the blanket by her legs suggesting Surtsey come closer but she stayed where she was, scared her mum would see the truth. 'They don't know, maybe a rockfall during yesterday's quake. Maybe something worse.'

Louise took a suck on the oxygen mask by her bed, her thin arm barely managing to lift it. She dropped the mask, picked up a tissue and coughed into it. She leaned back on her pillows and stared at the ceiling. She struggled to get breath, the rattle in her chest impossible to shake. She held up a hand like she was trying to stop time. 'Was it you who found him?'

Surtsey closed her eyes for a second and prayed for another earthquake.

'One of the other students. Tom was in the cove on the northwest, round from the jetty. We were taking samples on the eastern cliffs.'

'Oh, Sur.' Louise's hand wavered above the blanket, threadbare sunflowers stretched underneath. 'Come here.'

Surtsey took her hand and held it. It felt like her mum was barely there, her limbs twigs, her skin just dried leaves. There was no weight to her at all. Surtsey remembered Tom's weight upon her, the solidity of him as they lay naked on that stupid island a month ago, fucking in the open air, sand scrubbing at her back as she came in time with his final thrusts. She'd yelled out to the wind, believing there was no one for miles.

'I'm sorry you had to go through that,' Louise said.

Surtsey laughed despite herself. 'There are worse things going on.'

'It's not good for you, all this death.'

Surtsey sighed. 'I don't mind, I like coming to see you.'

'I meant Tom.'

Surtsey examined her mum, the deep crevices in her face, the yellow of her skin. The smell she gave off, ammonia and earth, like she was returning to the elements.

'He was a good man,' Louise said. 'Always tried to do the right thing.'

Surtsey wondered about that.

'How has Alice taken it?' Louise said.

Surtsey felt a tightness across her forehead and shoulders. She stretched her neck like a diver ready to jump.

'I don't know,' Surtsey said. 'We only just got back ourselves.'

'Poor woman,' Louise said. 'Having to tell the girls, too, I can't think of anything worse.'

Surtsey thought about the cameras on the prom. Had anyone seen her take the boat out or bring it back? What about satellite imaging or cameras on the firth? What about the imaginary blind date that she fed Halima?

She looked at Louise, at their hands together. Louise was staring out the window, east to the bump of Berwick Law. Her eyes were wet, maybe tears, but then her eyes were always wet, as if the last of her body fluids were desperate to escape. Louise was in a nappy the staff changed every few hours. Surtsey had to do that before Louise came here. Louise had been disgusted by the whole situation but the truth was that Surtsey didn't mind, didn't feel it dehumanised her mum. Just the opposite, it felt like a chance to repay her for bringing her up, a chance to demonstrate love. That seemed ridiculous and she never said it to Louise or Iona, but part of her was glad she'd been able to show how much Louise meant to her before she was gone.

Louise removed her hand from Surtsey's and wiped at her own cheek. Definitely tears. Surtsey closed her eyes and felt the warm flush to her face as her own tears came.

14

She walked home along the prom, flapping at her face with her hands to get the blood in her cheeks to calm down and clear the puffiness from her eyes. She walked past mums pushing buggies, kids on scooters, teenagers laughing and mucking about, cyclists zipping past on the commute home, all of it a blur. She usually found all this reassuring, it made her feel part of something. But right now she felt isolated, a membrane between her and the world.

'Hey, Sur, you OK?'

She hadn't even noticed Donna pushing an old lady in a wheelchair towards her.

'Hi.' She felt unable to carry out a normal conversation. Drunk and stoned, sad and angry, guilty. The day was too bright, the sun too warm on her skin, and she squinted.

Donna gave her a look of kindness, no trace of pity. Usually, when someone knew her mum was dying they acted all weird and distant. But Donna was different, a natural carer, none of the hang-ups. It had been a good choice for her to go into nursing, especially palliative care. She was strong, could handle the death and sadness.

The woman in the wheelchair was in her eighties, asleep with a tartan rug over her knees despite the buzzing evening heat.

'Jesse loves the sea air,' Donna smiled. 'But it sends her right over.'

Jesse was wearing a headscarf that made her look like a South American revolutionary. Maybe she had been. She was old enough to have done all sorts of things with her life. It was so easy to write her off as an old lady waiting for death, when she could've made love to Che Guevara in the jungles of Guatemala or argued over communism with Castro in the Cuban mountains.

Surtsey felt dizzy and closed her eyes.

'Maybe you should sit down,' Donna said.

Surtsey felt a hand at her elbow and let herself be led to the low seawall flanking the prom. She felt the grit of the sand under her hands as she placed them on the concrete and sat down. She opened her eyes. Yellow sand, not like the stuff on the island. How could two places so close be so different? But Surtsey knew the answer, she'd studied it for years, the reason behind rock types and formations, the rhythm of the planet she was standing on, trying not to float away.

They sat in silence. That was something else about Donna: she didn't feel the need to fill the void with blether, she knew when to just sit. It felt like people had been talking at Surtsey continuously lately, giving her no time to think, to gather herself and work out what to do.

A thin sliver of drool stretched from Jesse's mouth as she sat there. Donna reached out with a hankie and dabbed at it.

'How long have you worked at St Columba's?' Surtsey said.

'Over two years.'

'I couldn't do what you do.'

Donna smiled. 'Different folk are good at different things. I couldn't do what you do either.'

'Do you like it?'

'I love it.'

'Why?'

Donna considered for a moment. 'It's good to feel you're helping others.'

'But all the sadness,' Surtsey said. 'All the death in that place.'

'I like looking after people.'

'That's so admirable.'

'It is what it is.'

'But don't you wish you got more appreciation for what you do?'

'You don't do it for that. Helping people is its own reward.'

Surtsey shook her head. 'Do you believe in God?'

Donna laughed. 'Why do you ask?'

'I wondered if it made a difference. What you're talking about sounds like Christian goodwill.'

'I believe in something. I don't go to church but I think there is some force guiding us. Don't you?'

Surtsey thought of Tom, now in the morgue being picked over by professionals. 'No, I don't believe in anything like that. I wish I did.'

Donna reached over and touched Surtsey's hand. Surtsey was surprised at first, but it didn't feel weird, just comforting, and Surtsey squeezed Donna's hand back.

'It's just about doing the right thing,' Donna said.

'If only it was that easy.' Surtsey was surprised that she'd said that out loud.

Donna moved her hand away from Surtsey's on the wall and they sat in silence for a while.

Donna spoke, looking out to sea. 'Do you remember the first time we met?'

Surtsey searched in her memory. 'No, I don't think so.'

'I was in fourth year. I was down here at the beach with a group of folk. They weren't really friends, just folk who let me hang around with them. Denise, Lily and the rest. They were much more mature than me. It was end of term and everyone was drinking, there was a bonfire.'

Surtsey shook her head. If drink was involved, maybe that's why she didn't remember.

'Other groups were coming and going, drawn by the bonfire and bevvy. Denise was trying to impress some boy, I can't remember who, and started slagging me off to him and his mates, about my weight, telling them she'd seen me in the showers, the rolls of fat, it was disgusting.'

'She was a right bitch,' Surtsey said.

Donna smiled. 'You really don't remember this?'

Surtsey shook her head.

'Anyway, you were there with a couple of older girls. You were pretty drunk, and could've just sat there like everyone else, but you didn't, you stood up and tore strips off her, started shouting. She just shut up, ashamed she'd been called out. The boys looked awkward and drifted off.'

Surtsey laughed. 'Are you sure it was me?'

'I'm sure.'

'Doesn't sound like me.'

Donna turned and looked her in the eye. 'So you do know about doing the right thing, even if you don't think you do.'

Surtsey felt a shudder go through her and wondered if it was another aftershock.

'Did you feel that?' Surtsey said.

'What?'

'I just thought I felt something, a tremor.'

They sat on the wall, their fingers almost touching on the stone.

'Maybe I felt something,' Donna said, but Surtsey didn't know if she really had or if she was just making her feel better.

15

Sometimes you just needed to fuck a skinny Irish boy. Surtsey had spent the rest of the evening getting stoned with Halima in the living room as they compulsively watched the news. It was strange to be part of the story, dislocating somehow. When Halima had finally had enough and stumbled to bed, Surtsey felt suddenly lonely. So she made a booty call and, as if by magic, here he was in her bed.

There wasn't a scrap of meat on Brendan, barely any muscle either, just bone and sinew, all edges and bumps. They started off warm and fuzzy from the grass but Brendan could go for ages and gradually it woke Surtsey up, brought her more into the moment. She'd wanted to use him to forget about everything, but that was dishonest and disrespectful so she focussed and took charge, climbed on top, controlled the pace and rhythm, laughed out loud at simply fucking with no consequences. He came first but she was close behind, digging her nails into his scrawny arms as she felt the tremors through her.

She collapsed beside him on the bed.

He drank from a pint of water on the bedside table, Surtsey running a finger down his knobbly spine. She couldn't help comparing the two of them. With Tom she felt grown up, a real woman, whereas the juvenile joy of this was liberating. She felt physically different relative to the two men. With Brendan she became the curvy earth mother compared to his spindly frame. With Tom she felt like a sylph, a whisper of a woman compared to his bulk and experience.

'Penny for them,' Brendan said.

Surtsey shook her head and smiled. 'Just thinking how much I fancy you, that's all.'

'Back at you.'

They looked in each other's eyes for a time then Surtsey turned away, padded to the toilet.

In the bathroom she sat and made herself pee. She wiped and washed her hands, looked in the mirror of the bathroom cabinet.

'What are you doing?' she whispered to her reflection.

She opened the cabinet and saw creams and lotions, some of her mum's old stuff that she hadn't taken with her up the road. She thought about her mum asking for pills. She couldn't blame her. Surtsey wouldn't be half as brave in the circumstances. It took guts to make that decision.

She walked back to her room. Brendan lay on the bed with his eyes closed.

'I'm not asleep,' he said.

'Go ahead.'

He opened one eye. 'It's OK if I stay over?'

'Of course.'

'I just thought...'

'What?'

He propped himself up on his elbows. It was hard to take him seriously with his cock limp against his thigh.

'You seemed really upset in the pub,' he said. 'I didn't know if you wanted company.'

'You're here, aren't you?'

Brendan held her gaze. 'We're all right, aren't we?'

'How do you mean?'

'You and me.'

Surtsey put on a smile. 'Sure.'

'You'd tell me if there was something wrong?'

'Of course.'

'Good. Because I'm right into you, you know.'

They hadn't used the L word yet. So unlike Tom, who said it on their second night together, despite his family. Crazy way to speak but it meant different things to different people, who was she to judge. She didn't know if she loved Tom, or Brendan, if she'd loved any man. Or maybe she loved them all. How can you ever know yourself with all the noise and interference coming from the world?

She'd been seeing Brendan for over a year, a fact that shocked her every time she remembered. He'd done his undergrad at Trinity College while still living at home with his parents, pitched up in Edinburgh for his PhD at the same time as she started hers, desperate to get some independence. It was odd that he was living away from home for the first time just as she returned home to take care of her mum. They skirted around each other to begin with, just two faces in a group of friends, but gradually Surtsey began to notice his smile, the languorous way he walked, his easy grace. They snogged while drunk, then just kept going, never giving it a name, not hiding it but not displaying it either, drifting casually into a relationship. But Surtsey had never truly invested in it, that's why she was shocked it had gone on so long. She'd never met his parents or been back to Ireland with him, had barely met any of his friends, only knew the highlights reel of his childhood on the outskirts of Dublin with two older sisters. Maybe they were the reason he was so respectful of Surtsey, so un-macho. He was easy to like, very easy to fuck, but she was never sure that he was easy to love.

'Go to sleep,' she said.

'Coming to bed?'

She scrambled over him, kissed him on the way, stroked his thigh then settled in behind to spoon him.

It only took a couple of minutes for his breathing to become heavy and nasal. She uncurled herself and looked around the room as if she was a stranger, an interloper in her own life. The rickety old pine bed she'd picked up on Freecycle, plain white sheets. The dresser by the window, a clutter of make-up and toiletries, hand cream, anti-perspirant, overpriced Dior Poison Girl that smelt of bitter fruit. She remembered the tagline for the advert: 'I am not a girl, I am Poison.' The usual pretentious nightclub scenes, a doe-eyed model breaking society's rules. Such bullshit. And yet there was the bottle staring at her.

She went over and sat on the stool at the dresser. Lifted the glass stopper and dabbed at her neck. She wondered what would happen if she drank the contents. She gazed at the walls. No posters of singers or movie stars, but a large map of the world with pins in it for each country she'd visited. Fifteen so far, not bad but she hoped plenty would follow. One pin stuck in Iceland, when Louise had taken her as a teenager on a field trip to Surtsey, somehow circumventing visiting restrictions. She tried to remember the island but it merged in her memory with the Inch.

Elsewhere on her walls were posters of Surtsey and the Inch, and other new volcanic islands off the coasts of Indonesia and Japan. Another large poster of Yosemite, just to show she wasn't only obsessed with islands, and one of the Grand Canyon. No pin in the map for either of them yet. So much left to do, so many places to see.

An electronic ping she recognised sent a shiver through her. It came from her clothes piled up on the floor. Tom's phone. She reached for her jeans and pulled it out, swiped the screen. Another message from an unknown number:

I'm sorry.

She stared at the phone shaking in her fist. Brendan rolled onto his back, chest rising and falling. She watched him as he rubbed at his nose then relaxed.

Another ping in her hand:

I didn't mean it.

She wanted to throw the phone at the wall, smash it into a million pieces. Instead she just stared at the four words on the screen. She imagined it was the island itself, apologising for taking her lover from her. As if. She typed in reply:

Tell me who you are.

She pressed send and waited. Looked at the world map on the wall. Seven billion people on the planet, only one of them on the other end of this phone.

Ping:

Not yet.

She thought about that for a long time then replied:

Then when?

No answer. The phone screen eventually faded to black. Surtsey woke it up and typed:

If you're really sorry, go to the police.

A reply came quickly this time.

I can't. Goodbye.

'Wait,' she said. Brendan snuffled and scratched at his chest, murmured under his breath.

She pulled on joggers and a T-shirt, took the phone downstairs in the dark. She went into the living room but Iona was asleep on the sofa, leather jacket wrapped around her shoulders. She went into the kitchen then out the back door and stood in the garden on the small square of grass and tried to return call but no joy. Eventually she typed:

You coward. Who are you?

The light from the screen illuminated her face in the gloom. Her feet were wet from the dewy grass. She looked around as if she would find answers, saw the thin outlines of her neighbours' houses, the back wall that led to the lane, the shed where her boat slept.

She went to the shed and opened it, checked on the boat. It was as she'd left it, motor pulled up, hull locked into the trailer. She ran a hand along the side of the hull, rubber sticky against her fingers. Her hand came away sandy and she stared at it then wiped it on her trousers.

She looked one last time at the phone screen but knew there would be nothing. She put it in her pocket and pulled herself up into the boat. She landed inside and sat there, waiting for something to happen. Waiting for answers. Waiting for whatever was coming next.

16

'Found her.'

Iona's voice. Light lancing in through the shed door. Surtsey scrunched her eyes and sat up. Her back ached and her neck was stiff. She raised her hands straight up like she was praying, then slid her palms along her shoulders, her body creaking as she stretched.

'And you think I'm the unstable one,' Iona said.

'I don't think that.'

Iona was silhouetted in the doorway like an avenging angel. 'Sure you do. But I'm not the one sleeping in the boatshed.'

Surtsey pushed the blanket aside and sat up. She saw the mobile phone on the seat next to her and slipped it into her pocket as Iona offered her a hand to get out.

'What's going on, Sur?'

'Nothing.'

Surtsey clambered out, stumbling on the motor block, still half asleep.

'OK,' Iona said. 'That's why your boyfriend and BFF have been running around for half an hour looking for you. And that's why you're sleeping in a boat.'

Surtsey rubbed her eyes and looked outside. Cloudless sky, calm. 'I couldn't sleep last night so came out to get some air. Ended up here. No big deal.'

'Whatever.'

'I was drunk and stoned.'

Iona smiled. 'That's more like it. Speaking of which I'm making Bloody Marys for breakfast. Want one?'

Surtsey shook her head. Her hand went to her leg, felt the phone in her pocket through the material.

'Suit yourself,' Iona said, swaggering out of the shed.

As soon as she was gone Surtsey took the phone from her pocket. No messages.

'Hey.' Halima was at the door, still in her pyjamas.

Surtsey put the phone away. 'Hey.'

'You OK?'

'Fine.'

Halima raised her eyebrows. 'This is me you're talking to, not skankypants.'

Surtsey sighed. 'I just fell asleep.'

'Out here?'

'Maybe I was shaken up by yesterday, that's all.'

Halima rubbed Surtsey's arm. 'Don't make a habit of it. Brendan has been panicking since he woke up and you weren't there.'

'I'm allowed to do things without him.'

'He was just worried,' Halima said. 'You seem a bit spaced.'

Surtsey laughed. 'That's thanks to your grass.'

Halima held her hands out. 'Fair point.'

'Where's Brendan now?'

Halima nodded past the house. 'He went along the beach, thought you might've gone for a walk to clear your head.'

'That's not a bad idea.'

'He tried calling but you didn't have your phone with you.'

Surtsey resisted the urge to touch Tom's mobile in her pocket. Had Halima seen her slip it in there when she came in?

'I'll go find him,' she said.

*

She didn't bother to get changed, just threw her old hoodie on and tied her hair up in a bun. She called him but he was way along at the west end by the amusements. She padded up the prom in her crocs, staring at the phone messages from last night. She stopped at the green van and got two coffees then slipped through the gap in the sea wall and onto the sand. The prom was busy with commuters, cyclists, old folk heading to the swimming pool, in comparison the beach was nearly empty. The tide was way out and she scuffed down to the wet sand, squishing the squirmy piles left by lugworms, squelching over bladder-wrack. There was something about being the first one to spoil a stretch of flat sand, to leave your mark. She looked at her trail of footprints and thought about the sand on the Inch, her walk away from Tom's body. Below high tide, no trace. Maybe.

She saw Brendan at the groyne at the bottom of Bath Street, held the two coffees up for him to see.

When she reached him he put on a self-deprecating smile. 'There you are.'

Surtsey tilted her head and handed him a cup. 'Here I am.'

'I was worried sick.' He was joking, laughter in his voice, but she could tell he really had been worried.

She sipped coffee and linked her arm through his as they walked back along the sand. A handful of mallards were bobbing on the water. They looked too small for the expanse of the firth. The Inch was over to their left, a thin haze stretching from Burntisland and blurring its edges, making it more like a ghost than a solid presence.

'It's mad to think we were out there yesterday,' Surtsey said.

'Is it?'

'How many millions of tons of water are in the Forth, do you think?'

'I've no idea.'

'Do you think there will ever be other new islands?'

'Maybe.'

There had been several major eruptions since the Inch was born but none had created landmass above sea level. Each had formed under-water humps that meant shipping channels had to be changed, and maritime authorities constantly checked and updated their maps as volcanic matter eroded or shifted. Most ships avoided the southern side of the firth altogether, heading north around Inchkeith on their way to the oil terminal.

'Imagine the land always changing under your feet,' Surtsey said.

'What?'

'If none of this was solid, if the land shifted and moved.'

'It does,' Brendan said. 'It's called geology. It's what we study.'

Surtsey smiled and shook her head. 'No, I mean all the time, like the tides. If we woke up in the morning and everything outside the window had changed, the landscape altered when we weren't looking, all the maps of the world constantly out of date. What if we didn't know the shape of the world at all, how would we do anything? How would we know where we were?'

Brendan stopped walking and Surtsey did too, their arms still entwined.

'Are you sure you're OK?' Brendan said.

'I wish people would stop asking that.'

Something caught Surtsey's eye, a dozen people clustered around the boat lock-up next to the Beach House. A couple of police officers appeared at the end of Bath Street and headed towards them in no hurry.

Surtsey began walking towards the activity, Brendan in her wake. She trudged up the sand leaving deep heel prints, slowing as she hit the dry sand.

It was the Children of New Thule protesting by the fenced-off yard where the Edinburgh Uni boat was stored, along with all the boats and kayaks of the sailing club. Two young women were chained to the gate, stopping someone getting in. Red paint had been thrown through the chain links of the fence, splattered on the grass, streaked across three boats, including the Geophysics Department one. The police were shaking their heads, speaking into radios, fingers tucked under armpits. They were wearing too many clothes for summer. One of the cops approached Bastian, standing to the side of the rest. Surtsey noticed that he hadn't chained himself to anything.

As she came off the sand onto the promenade she recognised the cop speaking to Bastian, it was Ferris from yesterday, the tall cute one.

'Hey,' she said.

Ferris turned and looked surprised. 'Surtsey, right?'

That name always got remembered. Or maybe it was her flirting that stuck in his mind.

She realised now that the other cop was the female one from the Inch yesterday too. She was on the radio trying to arrange for someone with bolt cutters to come and get the women off the gate. The guy with the keys was on his phone too, relating the incident to his boss, most likely. A small smattering of people drinking breakfast coffee at the tables outside the Beach House next door were eyeballing the whole thing, a piece of extra street theatre to keep them entertained.

'Are you going to arrest these idiots?' Surtsey said.

Ferris scowled at her. 'We're handling it, thank you.'

Surtsey pointed at Bastian. 'Have you asked him about Tom.'

Bastian looked amused.

The cop was confused. 'Why would I do that?'

'He's a suspect.'

'Why?'

Surtsey pointed at the protest, the whole scene. 'Are you nuts? They want the Inch left alone, so a dead body found there is pretty handy for them.'

'That's a little far-fetched, don't you think?' Ferris said.

'Thank you,' Bastian said.

'Shut your face,' Surtsey said.

She thought about last night's texts and turned to Ferris. 'Check his phone.'

Ferris shook his head. 'I'm not doing that.'

'Go on, you might find something.'

Ferris held a hand up to Surtsey's arm, ushering her away.

'At least ask him his whereabouts,' Surtsey said, shrugging him off.

'Please leave the police work to us,' Ferris said. 'Thank you.'

So the flirting thing hadn't made a difference after all.

Bastian moved closer to the cop. 'If you want to investigate anyone, it should be her. She assaulted me on the beach yesterday.' He opened his palm to take in the crowd around them. 'I have many witnesses.'

Ferris sighed. 'Look, I'm not investigating anyone. I'm just a PC. We're here to get these women off the fence and let this guy do his job, that's all.' He turned to Surtsey. 'I'm sure the DCI will be looking at all possible leads in the case.' Then he faced Bastian. 'And unless you seriously want to press charges for assault, I suggest you shut up too.'

Surtsey stood staring at Bastian, who looked as smug as ever.

Ferris put his hand back on her arm. 'Now, if you could move along please, Miss.'

Surtsey shook her head, but let herself be guided away by Brendan, who she'd only just realised was there beside her.

She walked away reluctantly, glancing back at the scene, trying to make sense of it all.

'What a bunch of idiots,' Brendan said. 'You don't really think they're involved, do you?'

They were twenty yards away now.

Surtsey shrugged. 'Why not? Someone has to be.'

'Do they?' Brendan said. 'It could just have been an accident.'

Surtsey thought about the texts on the phone in her pocket. The messages from the Inch itself. It was sorry to have taken a life. It knew everything about her and Tom.

'Yeah,' she said. 'I suppose it could've been an accident.'

She looked back and saw Bastian talking to the female police officer, hands out in supplication. People passing by were slowing down to watch, herding their children away from the strange people making a disturbance. The boatyard guy was complaining to Ferris now but getting nowhere. Somehow this would all get sorted out, Surtsey thought. If everyone just communicated the world would sort itself out, maps would stay the same and we would all know what we were meant to do.

17

She stared at the spectral analysis numbers on her laptop. Three pages of spreadsheet, six columns of data, some secret hidden amongst the digits. That was one of the things she usually liked about her work, pulling meaning from seemingly random information, filtering the raw chaos of the universe into something you could understand. But some chaos couldn't be filtered, couldn't be made any sense of.

The data was about the relative density of a certain type of tuff within the rock samples they'd taken. It should give an idea about how this volcano had behaved on eruption, and that could be compared to other eruptions around the world. Was the Inch like the others, or unique? She wanted it to be a one-off but that's not the way science worked. What you wanted didn't come into it, you had to make sure not to skew the information with your own bias.

She looked at the clock in the corner of the screen. She'd been staring at the same page of numbers for twenty minutes. She wondered if she'd ever get back to normal, ever get the picture of Tom's sandy body out of her mind. If she would ever finish this PhD and get on with her life.

Tom's empty office didn't help. It was a black hole sucking in attention from all students and staff, their dead boss a presence because of his absence. Surtsey smiled at the paradox. It was the kind of thing she would've shared with him over a drink after work in one of the bars at the other end of town they used to go to, the boutique hotels in Stockbridge and New Town that felt like a different planet to the salty breeze of Joppa or the student-filled Southside.

The office around her was quiet, just Kez, Halima and Brendan clacking away on social media or answering emails, doing as much work as she was. She needed to focus, the numbers in front of her were the only way to get through this, a distraction from the shitstorm, something concrete she could hold on to.

She stared out the window at nothing, birch and oak rustling, wood pigeons flapping, traffic wheezing up and down West Mains Road.

She heard her email ping and turned back to the screen. It was probably just the usual junk from some geophys blogger, but she was conditioned to check by the noise. The email was from an address she didn't recognise, and when she read it she froze. It was from The.Inch@gmail.com, and the subject was 'Tom Lawrie and Surtsey Mackenzie'. She could see there were three jpegs attached, could make out the top of her own head in the first one already in the preview of the email. She felt like someone was controlling her finger as she clicked on the email to open it large on her screen.

And there they were, her and Tom, standing kissing outside the Roxburgh Hotel on Charlotte Square, her in one of her little summer dresses, him in a blue shirt, jacket and jeans. It was from two weeks ago, they'd been out for dinner in a new place on George Street round the corner, and were heading back to the hotel for a couple of hours of pretty feisty sex if Surtsey remembered correctly. They were just buzzed enough from the wine at dinner to be all over each other in the street, right when the picture was taken from across the road, by the looks of it.

The second picture was from a few moments later, both of them pulling back to look in each other's eyes after the clinch, sharing an intimate joke or comment, Surtsey laughing and throwing her head back, Tom with clear devotion in his eyes, like he couldn't believe his luck. The third picture had them with their arms around each other, Tom with his hand resting gently on Surtsey's buttock as they walked up the steps into the front door of the Roxburgh like a normal couple after a night out.

She looked at Tom's face in the second picture, it captured so well how he looked at her, why she had kept things going. Such a stupid ego boost, being adored like that by someone with authority just for being yourself, such a selfish reason to fuck him and fuck everything up.

Her heart was racing as she scrolled up and down through the pictures, she couldn't stop looking, remembering that night, the way they'd laughed at how bad his pork belly was in the restaurant, the cheesecake she'd made him order with two spoons, the single malt whiskies they'd had with coffee afterwards, joking about how he shouldn't get too drunk in case he couldn't perform later. Not that that was ever a problem, the sight of her was enough to get him hard in their room, and she knew exactly what to do to keep him going.

It was like he was back from the dead, and for a moment she imagined she would look up and see him sitting at his desk, smiling at her.

She checked the email for any more information but it was just these three pictures, no text. She checked the email address it came from again, and only then realised there were other addresses in the CC line. Halima, Brendan, Rachel. She clicked to show the rest of the addresses and her breath caught in her chest. Everyone in the department was on the list, then two more email addresses at the end, Alice.Lawrie@ gmail.com and Jason.Yates@scotland.pnn.police.uk.

Holy shit. His wife.

She thought for a moment, couldn't work out the last one, then it registered. DCI Yates, the cop investigating Tom's death.

No.

She stood up and her chair went flying behind her. Halima was staring at her with wide eyes, as was Kezia. Brendan was already heading towards her desk.

'What the fuck, Sur?' he said, his eyes wet already.

'Wait, Brendan, I can explain.'

He was at her desk now, fizzing with anger. 'Oh please. Don't you fucking dare say it's not what it looks like.'

Surtsey looked down at her desk for a moment, then realised the pictures were still on her computer screen. She wanted to click them away, but that would be crazy now, pointless.

Brendan had a hand on her desk, knuckles pressed against the wood. 'You were fucking him?'

Surtsey shook her head, just a tiny movement.

'You weren't fucking him? Is that what you're saying?'

Surtsey lifted her head. 'It wasn't like that.'

'Oh really? Just what was it like, Sur?'

She didn't speak. His body was leaning towards her, and she wondered for a moment if he would lift his fists from the table and hit her.

'Well? What the fuck was it like?'

Halima was out of her seat but standing back, look of amazement on her face.

Surtsey felt tears come to her eyes.

Brendan's face turned hard. 'Fuck off, you don't get to cry.'

He stood watching her in disgust.

'Unbelievable.'

He turned and walked out the office and down the corridor without looking back.

Kezia stood across the room, eyebrows just about at the roof.

Surtsey turned to Halima. With the light from the window behind her Surtsey couldn't make out her expression, but her hands were clasped together like a prayer.

'Holy shit, babes,' she said. 'Holy fucking shit.'

Surtsey grabbed her bag from under the desk.

'I have to get out of here,' she said.

18

Her feet pounded on the pavement, taking her out of King's Buildings and up the road to Blackford Hill. The adrenaline in her veins made her shake and she dabbed at the tears in her eyes, felt her breath jolt and shudder as she tried to compose herself. She turned off at Craigmillar Park golf course and up the steep slope, past the last few houses then she was at the old observatory with its green copper dome, building work along one side for a new lecture theatre. She went round to the right and up the grassy slope till she got to the trig point, then stopped, wheezing at the effort, and looked out over the city.

Incredible views from here, the castle sharp against the sky, Fife lurking behind. She could see the new bridge over to the left, the Pentlands behind her, Arthur's Seat, East Lothian, miles and miles of land, hundreds of thousands of people, lives just trundling along, people minding their own business, getting through as best they could.

She tried to think as her breathing regulated. A couple of crows were hopping about on the grass close by, looking for worms. She could smell the gorse blossom from the yellow bushes down the slopes, weirdly like a sharp version of coconut.

So everyone knew. Hal, Brendan, Alice. The police. The rest of the department.

Was this the same person as the one sending the texts to Tom's phone? If so, it meant that whoever it was had been following her and Tom around for a while now, at least two weeks. Why?

She looked out over the view to the north, the spread of expensive houses directly below, fanning out from the pond at the base of the hill. Tom's house was down there, in Mortonhall Road, easy walking distance to KB. She thought about Alice down there, sitting at her kitchen table, a mug of tea, opening her laptop to find that email. Or maybe that's not how it played out. Maybe Alice wasn't surprised at all by this news. Maybe Alice was behind it.

Surtsey stood there for a long moment, then began running down the hill.

*

15 Mortonhall Road was a fresh-faced Victorian semi with high hedges and sturdy gates leading into a smooth driveway. A builders' van was parked in the street and a large skip sat outside the garage, full of old bits of tiling, a toilet, hand basin and bath. The front door was open and two workies in overalls were carrying packets of tiles inside.

'You after Mrs Lawrie, love?' the older one said.

Surtsey steeled herself. 'Yeah.'

The old guy nodded. The younger one looked Surtsey up and down and smiled at her.

'I'll let her know,' the older one said. 'She's inside.'

Surtsey didn't know why she was here. Except she had to be. She had to face this down eventually, why not now?

She heard the guy shouting inside. 'Mrs L? Someone to see you.'

Part of her had hoped Alice wouldn't be in, would be off doing whatever grieving widows did. She looked behind her along the drive-way to the road, thought about running away, but her feet wouldn't move underneath her.

Alice came to the doorway holding a glass of white wine. Surtsey resisted the urge to look at her watch, but it was definitely still morning. But who the fuck was she to judge anyone else?

Alice wore black designer jeans, tight, showing off great legs, a sky blue shirt and navy blue jacket. Her blonde bob was shiny, her eyes red. She stopped and stared when she saw Surtsey.

'You,' she said. She took a big swig of wine. 'Wow, you've got a lot of nerve.'

'Excuse me.' This was the older builder, squeezing past and back out to the van in the street.

Alice waved her hand up the stairs behind her. 'Getting a new bathroom fitted. Although Christ knows how we're going to pay for it now. Listen to me, "we", there is no "we" any more.'

Surtsey's mouth was dry, and she had to peel her tongue from the roof of her mouth to speak. 'I'm sorry about Tom.'

Alice narrowed her eyes. 'Really? That's all you've got? You were fucking my husband and you're sorry?'

'So you got the email.'

Alice shook her head. 'Christ almighty.'

The workman excused himself past again, leaving the smell of plaster dust and an awkward silence in his wake.

'You don't seem very surprised,' Surtsey said eventually.

'I am so close to putting this glass in your face right now.'

'Well, you don't.'

Alice sighed. 'You think I didn't know already? I've loved him for twenty-four years, since you were in fucking nappies. You think I didn't know he was up to something? My God, it was obvious. The spring in his step, the extra workload, suddenly looking after himself. So many clichés. Every women's magazine in the world tells you to look out for the same signs, for Christ's sake. I didn't know it was you specifically, but what difference does it make now?'

Surtsey frowned. 'Did you send the email?'

Alice went bug-eyed. 'Are you insane?'

'Maybe you were following him. Following us.'

'I have better things to do with my time than follow my husband around. For a start, trying to keep this family together. So much for that.'

Surtsey took a deep breath. 'Maybe you killed him.'

Alice slapped her hard across the cheek. Surtsey saw the hand coming but didn't do anything to stop it.

'How dare you,' Alice said. She was glassy-eyed from the wine, or maybe crying. 'Gracie and Belle don't have a dad any more. Do you want to come back after school and explain to the girls why their daddy is never coming home?'

Surtsey shook her head. 'Have you been texting me?'

Alice stared icily at her. 'What the hell are you talking about?'

'Nothing.'

Alice put a hand on the doorframe, maybe to steady herself. 'All I know is that you were fucking my husband, and now he's dead.'

'That's not my fault.'

Alice went to close the door, the conversation was over.

'Isn't it?' she said.

19

DCI Yates looked as if he'd always been old. The gut, the pock-marked skin, the slump of his shoulders. Surtsey tried to picture him as a young boy chasing a football or flying a kite in the Meadows. Her mind came up blank.

Yates and another cop were sitting in her living room, bulky uniforms and jackets on despite the warm day outside. Surtsey had hoped to see Ferris, but he was obviously just a lowly uniform grunt. This other cop was younger than Yates but not by much, pale flesh in a double chin, thick, stubby fingers. The two of them were like something from last century, an anachronism. They were probably no older than Tom but seemed like a different species, dinosaurs still roaming the earth. As if to highlight their old-fashioned nature Yates had a small notepad and pencil out. He actually licked the pencil before he started writing.

'Let's start at the beginning,' he said.

Surtsey sighed and looked out the window. The rowing club were out on their afternoon training session, the green seven-seater easing through the calm of the Forth. She watched the rhythm of their oars for a few strokes, tried to breathe in time with it, but they rowed too slowly for her racing heart. She had to decide. Tell them everything and implicate herself, or tell them as little as possible, damage limitation.

She turned to Yates and the other cop. His name badge said Flannery. Flannery and Yates sounded like a bad vaudeville act or failed solicitors. They were squeezed into the sofa, cups of tea on the low table in front of them. Surtsey and Halima got stoned on that sofa last night, and she wondered if there were any threads of grass spilt down the sides. She had a quick panic, scanned the room for the hash pipe and ashtray, but saw nothing.

'Well?' Yates said.

Flannery had a sheaf of papers in his chubby fist. He hadn't shown them to her, but she assumed they were pictures of her and Tom.

'We were seeing each other,' Surtsey said.

'We know that,' Flannery said, giving the papers a shake. 'Since when?'

'Six months.'

Flannery pursed his lips.

Yates wrote in his pocket book. 'Tell us how it started.'

She kept it as dry and factual as possible but it still felt seedy, talking about her relationship to two strangers, two middle-aged men who would give their back teeth to have someone like her interested in them. Two fat old bastards who would probably wank off in the police station toilets thinking about it. It was a kind of abuse, having to detail her interactions with Tom, it debased the idea of the two of them. When they were together it had felt sincere, fun, innocent somehow. She realised how stupid that seemed as she talked about it.

She felt ashamed as they asked for details. The truth was she hadn't really cared about Alice and the girls, hadn't given them any thought while she grabbed Tom's hair as he went down on her.

Of course it was his fault as much as hers, in fact more so. He was the married one, for God's sake, the one being unfaithful. She imagined saying that to Alice: It's not my fault, it's your dead husband who slept with someone behind your back; he's the one who betrayed you and his children. He's the one thinking with his dick and not caring about the consequences.

She looked at Flannery and Yates. They were on Tom's side, men like them always would be. They might be having affairs too, using their position to impress or manipulate someone younger into sleeping with them. Wasn't that exactly what Tom had done? Surtsey bristled at the idea she was an innocent ingénue, swayed by his charm, but the more she talked about him the more it sounded like that's exactly how it was.

She ran out of words for the cops.

They gave each other a look as if they'd just smelt something rotten.

'And you didn't think to mention any of this on the Inch when his body was discovered?' Yates said.

Surtsey pictured Tom's body.

'I was in shock,' she said.

'Maybe you felt ashamed,' Flannery said.

'How do you mean?'

'Sleeping with a married man.'

'I'm not ashamed.'

'Guilty, then.'

'You don't get to judge me,' Surtsey said.

The temperature dropped a few degrees in the room.

Yates narrowed his eyes. 'We're just trying to establish the situation.'

'No, you're not,' Surtsey said. 'You're harassing me. Making moral judgements about my sex life. It's not relevant.'

'It's very relevant,' Yates said. 'It gives you a motive.'

'A motive for what? You don't even know if Tom was killed yet.'

'We're working on the presumption he was,' Yates said. 'Forensics should confirm it soon.'

'It doesn't give me a motive,' Surtsey said. 'I loved him.'

She was surprised to say it, but it felt like the truth.

Flannery's eyebrows shot up. 'So you loved him and he wouldn't leave his wife.'

Surtsey couldn't help rolling her eyes. 'Don't be ridiculous, I knew what I was getting into.'

Yates sucked through his teeth. 'It sounds like you didn't know what you were getting into, given that your married lover has just been found dead.'

'I shouldn't even have to say this but I had nothing to do with it.'

Yates moved his tongue around, like he was trying to dislodge food from his molars. 'Please tell us your whereabouts leading up to the discovery of Professor Lawrie's body.'

'I was at the Grant Building from about ten in the morning. Before that I went to see my mum at the St Columba's hospice up the road. Before that I was here with my housemate Halima and sister Iona.'

'And what about the day before he was found?'

'The same. At the hospice seeing mum in the morning, then the office all day, then back here.'

Yates watched her carefully. 'And you were at home for the whole evening?'

Surtsey thought about coming in the back door and meeting Halima in the kitchen. 'Yes.'

'Can anyone confirm that?'

Surtsey felt her leg tremble, tried not to look at it.

'Halima. I was here with her all night.'

'What did the two of you do?'

She thought about the grass, the red wine, the image of Tom in her mind, her wet dress from the sea spray, the saltiness on her lips.

'Drank wine and watched crap TV.'

'What did you watch?' Flannery said. He hadn't spoken in ages, and his voice unsettled her.

'Comedy stuff. *Parks and Rec, Kimmy Schmidt.*'

Yates diligently wrote that down in his book.

Flannery took a deep breath and shifted his weight on the sofa, making it creak.

Yates tapped the pencil against the pad, then closed it.

'We'll speak to your housemate and get back to you. Until then, try not to sleep with any married men.'

Surtsey dug a fingernail into her own leg to stop from blurting out a string of expletives.

The two men got up and headed for the door, trailing an air of entitlement.

Flannery was already in the hall when Yates turned in the doorway and fixed Surtsey with a look.

'Is there anything else you want to tell us, Miss Mackenzie?'

Surtsey held his gaze, blinked, and shook her head.

20

'Come on.' Surtsey listened to the burble of the phone ringing, five times then it went to voicemail.

Halima's recorded voice. 'Leave a message.'

'Hal, it's Sur, call me back soon as you can. It's super-urgent. Seriously.'

She scuffed over the sand and kicked at a rope of seaweed, releasing a squelch of liquid over her shoes.

'Shit.'

She looked along the beach. The tide was in, a soft shimmer of waves throbbing against the coast. The sky was gauzy, high haze diffusing the light into a veil over the world. The Inch was a spectre out there, Fife unknowable behind it. She squinted against the fuzzy brightness, longed to see a pillar of smoke driving up from the island, lava spewing from the vents. It was crazy but she missed the island even now. It was so much a part of her, integral to her life, that she couldn't bear to be away from it for too long.

She felt something under her feet. The sand seemed to vibrate and dance, a yellow blur all around. A gang of seagulls lifted up in a fluster and she felt the first jolt of the quake, a shudder that made her balance shift. She planted her feet, gazed around. Other beach walkers had stopped and done the same, waiting like statues for it to subside. That's all you could do. A rumble under her shoes as the ground shifted again, grains of sand chasing each other towards focus points, like hourglasses running out. Her fingers were splayed, knees bent like a surfer on a board trying to stay on the big wave. More shifts, a tip one way then the other, the seagulls high in the sky, the air silent like everyone was holding their breath. The shudders gradually subsided replaced by a tremble, a guitar string being plucked, a thin thrum that she felt up her legs and into her hips.

Then it was over.

Surtsey realised she really had been holding her breath. She sucked in air. That was more than just an aftershock. That was as big as the one she'd experienced on the Inch two nights ago. She hadn't heard any earthquake predictions on the news, but it was a hopelessly inexact science, guessing when earthquakes and volcanoes would fire into action. The earth wanted to keep humankind on their toes.

An old man walked past, highland terrier snuffling at Surtsey's ankles then scuttling off.

'Strong one, eh?' he said.

She watched the man as he walked away. She'd grown up with these disturbances her whole life but he knew a time before them, had spent most of his life on solid ground. She tried to think what that felt like.

She flinched at a ringtone in her pocket. She pulled out her own phone. She was carrying both phones now, in case there were more messages. But this was her phone ringing now. Halima.

'The earth move for you, babes?'

'Hal.'

'Sorry I never got back sooner, been in a dumb meeting with Rachel. "Keeping the ship steady in these turbulent waters," or some shit. What's the big panic?'

Surtsey pulled at her earlobe. 'I need your help.'

'I've got your back, you know that.'

'Good.' A pause. 'Have you spoken to the police yet?'

'Just on the island yesterday. Why?'

'They're coming to see you.'

'Right.'

Surtsey could hear the doubt in Halima's voice.

'I need you to lie to them.'

Static on the line for a moment. 'What's this about?'

A young mum was sitting with two toddlers along the beach, picnic blanket laid out. Sippy cups and sandwiches, a bunch of grapes. The kids were nonplussed by the recent quake but the mum threw Surtsey a worried look.

'They just interviewed me,' Surtsey said. 'About the whole Tom thing.'

'We seriously need to talk about that, by the way,' Halima said.

'We will, I promise. The cops asked me where I was the night before we found Tom.'

'You were out on a date.'

'I said I was at home with you the whole time.'

Silence. 'Why?'

Surtsey closed her eyes. 'I panicked. I didn't want them thinking... they already knew about me and Brendan, and me and Tom. I didn't want them to know I was out with someone else.'

Halima sighed. 'I don't know, babes.'

'These cops were dicks,' Surtsey said. 'Judging me, you know what it's like.'

'Still.'

Surtsey breathed in and out.

'Maybe you should go back and tell them the truth,' Halima said.

'I can't,' Surtsey said. 'I already feel stupid, I can't handle even more guilt.'

'I can't believe they're hassling you. Are they really suggesting you had something to do with Tom's death?'

'They're just fishing, they don't have a clue about anything. They didn't like me, that's for sure, because of my thing with Tom.'

'But this date guy is your alibi.'

Surtsey paused. 'No, you're my alibi now. OK?' She had her teeth clenched. She made an effort to ease the tension in her jaw. 'You said you've got my back, Hal.'

'Come on.'

'It's not like you need to lie. We did stay in that night drinking, watching TV. That's all you have to say.'

'Maybe miss out the part where we got monumentally stoned.'

Surtsey forced a laugh. 'Yeah.'

Halima's tone had shifted, she was on board. 'OK.'

'You'll do it?'

'I'll do it.'

The gulls had drifted back down and were pecking at the seaweed looking for food.

'But we need to talk about all this, Sur. Tonight, yeah?'

'Definitely.'

Halima ended the call and Surtsey put her phone away. She got the other phone out her pocket and stared at the screen. Flicked to Messages and read through the texts from last night. She scrolled through the other messages between her and Tom, arranging to meet at the Inch. They'd never explicitly mentioned the place, but Surtsey got her own phone back out and deleted all the messages between them. If the police took her phone they could presumably get that data back but it was all she could do for now.

She looked at Tom's phone. This was the key. Someone had been following them. She had to find out who, and what they wanted. Her thumb moved over the letters:

Come and get me, motherfucker.

She pressed send and looked up, stretched her neck, easing out the knots in her shoulders. In the distance one of the toddlers had run away from the picnic blanket and fallen face first into the sand. She picked herself up and continued tottering to the water's edge, her mum shadowing a few yards behind, looking out for her, keeping her safe from harm.

21

Iona was a natural behind the bar, like that was the only place she came alive. Kicking around the house she was surly or drunk, argumentative or morose, never communicating. But stick her between the beer pumps and the spirit gantry and she glowed with energy, chatting to other staff, flirting with regulars, rebuffing their jokes or tearing a strip off them if they went too far. She moved in a blur, wiping down the bar, clipping out change, slicing limes, stacking the glass washer, ducking out the way when they lifted the cellar trapdoor.

Surtsey watched her sister with narrow eyes. They used to get on when they were younger, Iona looking up to her big sister, trying to gain the secrets of make-up, boys and booze before she was ready. In return Surtsey looked out for her, stepping in to ward off playground bullies, holding her hand as they crossed the road, packing her gymnastics bag when she was running late for training.

She couldn't picture Iona doing gymnastics now. The only exercise she got was lifting a pint to her lips. She gave up everything when she hit fourteen, the hip-hop classes, the cheerleading, the basketball. Then when their mum was diagnosed Iona gave up everything else, including any attempt at civilised conversation. It was her way of coping but that didn't make it any easier. And it didn't help that Louise was so fucking forgiving about it. Why should Surtsey shoulder all the responsibility of visiting mum when she never got any credit for it? But she didn't do it for credit, of course.

Iona spotted her standing at the bar, beamed and came over.

'What brings you here this time of day? Don't you have volcanic mud to sift through?'

'You have such a deep understanding of my work.'

'I always listen when you bang on about rocks.'

'Shiraz, please.'

Iona poured a large one and handed it over. 'On the house.'

Surtsey raised her eyebrows. 'Thanks.' She glugged then sighed as the glass left her lips.

'Looks like you need it.'

'You have no idea.'

Iona checked the bar. Surtsey followed her gaze. A bald guy in his fifties with AC/DC and Aerosmith tattoos had a Sudoku book open, end of a pencil in his mouth. Elsewhere, two rosy-cheeked guys in red corduroy trousers were sipping pints of Guinness and laughing. At the fireplace a trio of young mums were stretching their boozy lunch to infinity, their kids clambering over each other on a sofa.

'Is this about your boss?' Iona said.

'Yeah.'

'Must be tough, someone you know dying.'

It hung in the air for an eternity, the echo of their mum.

'It's not just that,' Surtsey said.

Iona flipped a cloth between her hands, dabbing at a wet ring on the bar top. 'How do you mean?'

'You're going to find out anyway.'

'What?'

Surtsey took a drink, lowered her glass. The mums burst into laughter at the other end of the bar. Light played in through the window, dust giddy in the beams.

'I was sleeping with him,' Surtsey said.

Iona whistled. 'Wasn't he married?'

Surtsey nodded.

'Christ,' Iona said. 'I thought you knew better than that.'

Surtsey tilted the glass to her mouth, finished her wine and rolled the glass around in her hand. Iona grabbed the bottle and refilled it.

'It gets worse,' Surtsey said.

Iona didn't speak, just screwed the top back on the bottle.

Surtsey drank. 'The police know. His wife knows.'

Iona had her hands on the bar. 'Don't they have kids?'

Surtsey paused with her wine glass in mid-air. 'You're not helping.'

'Sorry.'

Surtsey took a breath. 'Two girls, Gracie and Belle, nine and six. Now without a dad.'

'That's not your fault.'

Surtsey laughed. 'Try telling the police that. They came to the house and interviewed me. Asked about my whereabouts. I might well be a suspect.'

Iona laughed. 'Jesus wept.'

'Glad you find it funny.'

Iona shook her head. 'It's just so...'

'I know.'

'You're the sensible one.'

'Apparently not.'

Iona got a wine glass down from above the bar and poured herself a glass. 'If one of us was going to have an affair with a married man, get found out by the wife and be a suspect in his death, I always presumed it would be me.'

Surtsey spluttered into her drink. 'Me too.'

Iona held out her glass. 'Cheers.'

'Cheers.'

They both took a big hit. Iona looked round and caught the eye of Metal Sudoku, who held his empty glass up. She poured an IPA and placed it in front of him, sharing a smile. She took the money and popped his change in the tips jar.

'Maybe we're having a *Freaky Friday* personality swap,' she said as she returned.

'Then you would be sensible,' Surtsey said.

'Well I'm at work, while you're drinking wine in the afternoon.'

Surtsey pointed. 'So are you.'

'Good point.'

Silence between them, not uncomfortable.

'You know I miss this,' Surtsey said.

'Drinking in the afternoon or sleeping with married men?'

Surtsey pressed her lips together. 'You know what I mean.' She held her hands open to indicate the two of them. 'Us talking.'

'We talk.'

'Not really.'

'What do you want to talk about?'

'Mum.'

Iona shook her head. 'You had to go there.'

'Come on.'

'What is there to say, Sur? Our mum is dying and there's nothing we can do and it's shit beyond words. Happy?'

'No.'

'Well, then.'

'But you're wrong, there is something we can do.'

Iona shook her head.

'We can make it easier for her,' Surtsey said. 'We can help her.'

'She's our mum,' Iona said. 'She's supposed to help us.'

'She needs us. Why won't you go and see her?'

Iona straightened her shoulders and picked up the bar cloth, smeared the already clean bar.

'It breaks her heart,' Surtsey said.

'You don't get to do this.'

'Do what?'

Iona squeezed the bar cloth. 'You don't get to nag me, to be the sensible one telling me what to do. We've switched personalities, remember, *Freaky* fucking *Friday*?'

'If you're the sensible one, be sensible.'

Silence.

'Go and see her,' Surtsey said.

Iona downed the last of her wine. 'Fuck you.'

'I know it's hard.'

Iona put her empty glass in the washer. One of the posh guys was at the bar getting the next round. Iona poured two Guinness, took the money while they settled. When she'd finished, Surtsey held her glass up by the stem, wiggled it.

'Can I get another?' she said. 'I'll pay this time.'

Iona sighed. She got the bottle and plonked it next to her sister. 'Just drink it. It's easier to lose a whole bottle of stock than a couple of glasses anyway.'

Surtsey poured it herself.

'Here you are.' The familiar accent made her turn.

Brendan stood with his fists shoved in his pockets, lines across his forehead.

'Here I am,' Surtsey said. The Shiraz had warmed her, the edges of the afternoon fuzzy. Her heart lifted at the sight of him, but her stomach tightened too.

'I don't know why I'm here,' Brendan said.

Surtsey stayed quiet.

Brendan lifted a hand to his hair.

Surtsey puffed out her cheeks. 'I'm so sorry.'

Brendan shook his head. 'How long?'

'Can I get you anything?' Iona said from behind the bar.

Brendan hesitated, looked at the lager and ale taps, confused. 'No thanks.'

Surtsey felt heat rise to her face.

'Well?' Brendan said.

'I don't know.'

'Yes you do. How long?'

'Why does it matter?'

'The details matter.'

She didn't want to discuss details because the details hurt the most, made it real.

'Six months.'

'Fuck's sake.'

'I'm sorry.'

'So you've said.'

'I am.'

Brendan ran his tongue around his teeth, chewed the inside of his cheek. 'You want to know the worst thing?'

'Brendan, don't do this.'

His voice was hard. 'Do you want to know the worst thing?'

Surtsey's heart was sore, tight.

Brendan put a hand out to the bar, just his fingertips, as if checking the world was tangible.

'The worst thing is that you'd still be fucking him behind my back if he hadn't died.'

'Brendan…'

'You didn't end it. He didn't end it. He fucking died, that's the only reason.'

Surtsey thought about saying sorry again but what was the point?

'I don't blame you for being angry,' she said.

He nodded, animated. 'Oh, you don't blame me? That's nice. That's lovely, thanks. I have your permission to be angry, I am so fucking honoured.'

'I didn't mean…'

'Shut the fuck up.' His voice was louder, making Metal Sudoku look over. 'Just shut the fuck up.'

Iona came over. 'Everything OK?'

Brendan had his arms by his sides, hands balled into fists. The tendons on his forearms twitched as he clenched.

'Did you know?' he said to Iona.

She shook her head.

He turned to Surtsey. She was gasping to take a drink of her wine.

'Did anyone know?'

'No one.'

Brendan tilted his head. 'That's nice, just you and Tom, cosy little lovebirds. Do you realise what a cliché you are? A student fucking her professor?'

'I think you should leave,' Iona said. 'Before you do something you regret.'

Brendan nodded at his fists then at Surtsey. 'Hit her? Is that what you mean?'

Surtsey wanted him to hit her. She'd felt relief when Alice slapped her, relief when Brendan and Kezia found Tom's body on the Inch. It was all following a path and she had no choice but to be swept along.

'Go,' Iona said.

Brendan stood silent for a moment then touched his forehead.

'The cops came to see me,' he said.

'Me too.'

'Asking about me and Kez finding Tom. What we were doing that whole day, and the day before.'

'I'm sorry.'

'You're sorry,' Brendan said under his breath. 'That's useful.'

He shook his head and put his hands back in his pockets. Iona watched.

'I thought I knew you, Sur,' Brendan said. 'I thought we had something.'

More silence. Nothing to say.

Brendan turned to leave. 'I hope he was worth it.'

He walked out the pub door.

Surtsey watched the door close and picked up her glass, had to use two hands to keep it steady as she downed what was left, feeling the burn spread down her throat and through her body.

22

Louise lay in bed with an untouched food tray in front of her. Stew of some kind, brown slop with dry mash and wrinkly corn on the side. Surtsey didn't blame her mum for not touching it and she felt heartburn from the red wine as she stared at the plate.

The television in the corner was on the news. A plane missing over the Indian Ocean, a politician having an affair, scaremongering about immigration. It was strange to see all the ordinary tragedies of life just trundling on as if nothing had changed. But Surtsey felt different, the steadiness of her life a couple of days ago had vanished, the ground under her feet was constantly shifting.

A reporter appeared walking across the sand of Portobello beach, speaking to camera. The sound was too low to make out what she was saying, but it would be the same stuff, police following lines of enquiry, appealing for witnesses.

Louise coughed into a tissue, folded it and placed it on the blanket, away from the food. 'Are they any closer to finding out what happened to Tom?'

Surtsey was sitting by the bed on a red plastic chair that dug into her thighs and rubbed against her spine. 'Mum, there's something I have to tell you.'

She wondered if she needed to. Louise was dying, maybe Surtsey could get away with never mentioning it. But she couldn't stay quiet, that's not how she was with her mum. They told each other stuff. She needed help.

Louise turned from the television screen to look at her daughter, but didn't speak.

'It's about Tom,' Surtsey said.

No reply, just waiting. Surtsey sometimes wondered if her mum could've been a psychiatrist, using emptiness to make people say stuff they wouldn't usually reveal.

Surtsey breathed in, felt her stomach grumble, the acid messing with her.

'I was...'

The television news had moved on, the screen now showing footage of chickens in cages. Something about the possible return of bird flu. Surtsey's own little drama was only a tiny snippet of the news agenda, filler for a couple of minutes. If only she could move on as easily as the broadcasters. What happened to all the stories in the world when the news teams got bored of them? Surtsey pictured countless people sitting and suffering with no one to tell their story to. The relatives of the air passengers lost in the ocean, the family of the MSP shagging around, the immigrants being sent back to Syria or Iraq or wherever because no one gave a shit.

Surtsey's face was hot. She placed the back of her hand against her cheek, her cool fingers felt nice. She'd always had bad circulation, something she shared with her mum, the two of them in thick socks and slippers around the house, blankets over their knees on the sofa as they snuggled in to watch the latest Netflix thing.

Surtsey looked out the window then down at her lap.

'I was seeing him,' she said, head down. She didn't want to look at her mum's face.

Silence for a while, so that she thought maybe Louise hadn't heard.

'Sleeping with him,' she said.

There was a long silence. 'Oh, Sur.'

'I know,' Surtsey said. 'A married man, old enough to be my father, what about his poor wife. You don't have to say any of it.'

She looked up, her eyes wet.

Her mum was staring at her, jaw tight. 'I wasn't going to say that.'

'You don't need to.'

Surtsey reached out and took Louise's hand. Shocking lack of flesh, like she was already just a skeleton in a thin bag of skin. She squeezed gently, her thumb in her mum's palm.

Surtsey wiped at her tears. 'Alice knows.'

'Oh, darling.'

'I deserve it.'

A long pause. Too long.

'Don't be too hard on yourself.'

'Why shouldn't I? I've been a fucking idiot.'

'We all do stupid things.'

'Not you,' Surtsey said.

Louise looked out the window. 'I've had my fair share.'

'Like what?'

Louise looked at the congealing food on the tray, took a sip from a water bottle. Swallowing looked like such hard work, Surtsey didn't know how her mum managed it. Louise put the bottle down with a trembling hand.

'Let's talk about something else.'

Surtsey touched her knuckles to her eyelids, the cold of her hand drawing the heat away from her face. 'Mum, what are you not telling me?'

'Nothing.' Louise picked at a loose thread on the blanket. 'When you come to the end of your life...'

'Mum.'

'...things reduce down. Like you've been simmering the whole time, reducing until there's only the essence left. All the rest of it.' Louise lifted a hand and waved at the bland decor. 'It's just distraction. Noise.'

She looked out the window. The haze from earlier had lifted and Fife was in sharp relief. Light glinted off the windows of the holiday homes at Burntisland, winks of life against the landscape.

'How's the boat?' she said.

Surtsey remembered waking up in it. Was that just this morning? 'It's fine.'

Louise turned. 'I'd like to go out in it.'

'I don't think so.'

'Why not?'

'You're not well enough for a boat trip.'

'Says who?'

Surtsey pointed at Louise's body under the covers and immediately regretted it.

Louise smiled. 'Are you going to deny a dying woman her last request?'

Surtsey snorted. 'Don't pull that "last request" crap, you'll be around for a while yet.'

'Maybe not.'

Surtsey felt her heart tighten. 'Have they said something?'

'Nothing like that.'

Surtsey narrowed her eyes. 'I can't get you into the boat on my own and you can't manage yourself, so how would we do it?'

'Iona could help, maybe.'

Surtsey sighed. 'When was the last time she came to see you?'

'Yesterday.'

Surtsey frowned. 'Really? She never mentioned it to me.'

'Your sister doesn't need to tell you everything.'

'What was she doing here?'

Louise looked at her. 'What a strange question, she came to see me of course.'

'She can't help anyway, she's working.'

Something came over Louise's face and she pressed the red button on her bed for assistance.

A few moments later there was a knock on the door and Donna came in.

'Not eating?' she said.

Louise shook her head. 'You know how it is.'

'You can manage a wee bit, surely?'

Louise pursed her lips. 'Donna, when do you finish your shift?'

Donna looked at her watch. 'Just under an hour. Why?'

'How would you like a boat trip?'

23

The wine had worn off and Surtsey's head felt tight, but once they got a few knots up the spray in her face and the wind skimming off the water slapped her awake. Louise sat in the prow, blankets already wet, the bulk of a lifejacket making her look more solid than she had in a long time. Surtsey was on the tiller, steering the boat into the brown-grey swells, not much in the way of waves today but it didn't take a lot to make them buck and bounce, the mass of water like brick under the hull, a shudder with every hit.

They were pointing northeast, the boat aiming for Berwick Law but really just getting distance from shore into the wide-open space.

Donna sat to Surtsey's right, gripping the rubber handles on the edge of the boat, feet wide apart.

'You OK?' Surtsey said.

'Fine.'

Louise looked more alive than Surtsey had seen her in ages. She regretted not having brought her out in the boat recently. Her mum loved the open water, loved islands, loved the remoteness and isolation and freedom. Why hadn't Surtsey taken her out here every bloody day? Because she was already used to the idea of Louise dying, she had already put her in a coffin and lowered her into the ground in her mind. It was a terrible thing to admit to herself.

'She seems happy,' Donna said, nodding at Louise.

'Yeah.'

'What about you?' She was shouting over the buzz of the engine.

'What about me?'

'How are you?'

'Fine.'

It was the standard answer. The word you never had to think about, let alone mean. Fine, fine, fine, fine, fine. When really you were terrified, miserable, confused, angry, hopeless.

Louise turned back to them. Her eyes were so bright Surtsey wondered if she'd taken something. Louise pointed west. Surtsey had been waiting for it, knowing all along what her mum wanted to do.

The Inch.

Without speaking Surtsey aimed the boat westwards in a loop.

Of course this was crazy. They didn't have permission to land, it wasn't an officially sanctioned boat, and it was still a crime scene.

'What are you doing?' Donna said, eyes narrow as the boat bounced over the wash.

Surtsey pointed. 'The Inch. Mum wants to see it.'

'We're not landing though?'

Surtsey shrugged. 'Have you been up close before?'

Donna shook her head and gripped tighter as the boat's nose flipped up then landed in a splash.

It always surprised Surtsey that other people weren't as obsessed with the island as she was. It was virgin territory, a brand new land, why wouldn't you want to explore it? And yet people walked along that beach every day and never gave it a second thought. Maybe folk took it for granted because it had been there for over two decades now, part of the scenery.

Surtsey could remember countless drunken conversations in pubs, usually with boys trying to get into her pants, where she tried to explain the attraction. Why she studied it, how it brought her closer to something elemental, a feeling she belonged. Of course no one belonged on the Inch except the birds who nested on the cliffs, the insects who made it their home, the grasses and mosses, the fragile ecosystem that had developed in two decades. They were the future of the Inch, the future of the planet. Surtsey thought of humanity as a blip, a tiny ecological anomaly that would soon be wiped away, leaving the earth to get back its equilibrium. Fanciful crap of course, humankind was fucking up the planet as best it could, but she wouldn't be sorry if they destroyed themselves before they destroyed the world.

They approached the southeastern cliffs where she'd collected samples the other day. Heaving grey slabs of land rooted in the sea. The cliffs contained tons of basaltic glass, formed when the magma from the original eruption cooled instantly, from twelve hundred degrees to zero as it hit the water. Steam explosions launched clouds and debris miles into the atmosphere. That the planet could so easily take on new forms, that's why she studied geology. On the one hand you looked at periods of time stretching for aeons, on the other, things could be created or destroyed in a moment.

Louise turned from the front of the boat and beamed at Surtsey and Donna. She looked so much younger, the years fallen from her face.

Surtsey slowed the engine and angled the boat to skim round the south cliffs where cormorants and terns were sunning themselves. She saw puffins nestling in crevices, and this year the first gannets had arrived from the Bass Rock colony downriver. They turned up the west coast, the vents visible from this side, two natural amphitheatres, black bowls of rock, one bigger than the other like a protective older sister. They reached the cove in the shadow of the peaks where Tom was found. Surtsey rubbed her eyes.

Louise was engrossed in the view, leaning forward and peering at the landscape, eyes wide, soaking it in.

Surtsey shot a glance at Donna. She wanted her to understand the power of this place, the effect it could have on you. That was the reason her and Tom had sneaked out here in the first place. It wasn't about the sex, though they had plenty of that. It was about inspiration, feeling insignificant in the face of it yet also part of something bigger. Surtsey never articulated this to Tom or anyone else. Right now she felt it again. It sounded hippyish, too much like her mum's Gaia earth mother routine. But it was true, she felt in touch with the universe here like nowhere else.

They were round the cove now and Surtsey saw the jetty.

Louise called back. 'Can we land?'

Surtsey looked at Donna.

'We're not allowed, right?' Donna said.

'Come on,' Louise said.

'I don't know,' Surtsey said.

Her mum looked at her, the tip of her tongue jammed between her teeth. 'Do I need to play the dying mum card?'

'Louise,' Donna said, shocked.

'Well, I'm dying, aren't I?'

'Don't,' Surtsey said.

'Don't die? I wish I had the choice.' She turned to Surtsey. Her shoulders were straighter than they'd been in months. 'I want to land.'

Surtsey thought about Tom, the police, the messages on her phone. She looked around.

'If you're sure,' she said.

Louise smiled then turned towards the island.

Donna frowned.

Surtsey gunned the engine and poked the boat towards the jetty. She lined up alongside, cut the engine then threw the towrope over the post and pulled the boat in.

Donna got off first to help Louise out. She and Surtsey each held one of Louise's hands and lifted her onto the jetty. Surtsey stepped out after, Donna giving her a hand.

Louise took a few hesitant steps along the planks, the girls hovering at either side.

'I can walk, for Christ's sake,' she said, shuffling forwards.

She held a post and stepped onto the black sand. She crouched in slow motion, using the post to help her. Surtsey watched. Her mum moved like someone twice her age. Louise touched the sand, scooped a handful and straightened up. She lifted the sand to her face and breathed in, a few grains falling from her fingers.

'I've missed this place,' she said.

Donna stood behind, ready to catch her if she stumbled. Surtsey wondered about Donna's relationship with Louise. Surtsey had looked after her as long as she could at home until it was too much. She loved that closeness, even in adversity. But she didn't believe that whatever doesn't kill you makes you stronger. Whatever doesn't kill you could still make you as weak as a newborn, it could destroy you in other ways, negate all the good in your life, leave you with nothing.

'I was first here twenty-four years ago,' Louise said. 'It was only a year old. You should've seen it back then. So full of energy, elemental.'

She was talking like the island was an old lover.

Surtsey had a flash of fucking Tom on the eastern lava flow, behind the research hut, the sky violet at sunset, a lemon moon emerging over the vents.

Louise touched the sand to her mouth and kissed it. Grains stuck to her dry lips.

'It was settling down,' she said. 'Maybe it still is. Maybe there will be more eruptions, more earthquakes. That's why I love this place.'

She looked around. The low sunshine was a warm bath of light, long shadows from the vents turning the rocks purple. It felt like the land was breathing, a heartbeat under the surface.

She brushed the sand from her fingers.

'It always surprises you. This place can do anything.'

24

'You have a beautiful home.'

Surtsey turned from pouring the wine. 'Thanks.'

She took the glasses over to the kitchen table where Donna was fidgeting with a bangle on her wrist.

They touched glasses. Surtsey took a couple of gulps as Donna had a sip.

'I don't actually drink very much,' she said.

'You don't know what you're missing.'

'It tastes nice,' Donna said, placing the glass on a coaster. 'But I don't like to get drunk.'

Surtsey snorted and took another drink. 'Christ, that's the best thing about it.'

They'd dropped Louise back at the hospice, exhausted but smiling. Maybe it hadn't been physically good for her, using up her reserves of energy, but Surtsey was sure it had helped her mental state, seeing her mum's face on the Inch made that clear.

Once they got her settled at the hospice, Donna and Surtsey left, then shared an awkward silence on the prom. Surtsey didn't want to be alone. Iona was working, Brendan was gone and she didn't know where Halima was. So she asked Donna back to the house, partly to say thanks for helping with Mum, partly for company. And partly because she felt she owed her something. The fact they hadn't really known each other at school seemed a missed opportunity now. She was easy to talk to, a good listener, and she was the only person in Surtsey's life at the moment who didn't know about her relationship with Tom. If she could keep a small pocket of her life insulated from that, all the better.

Surtsey pulled up the chair opposite Donna and sat down.

'I've walked past this house a hundred times on the way to work and never realised it was yours,' Donna said.

'Where do you live?'

'Across the other side of Milton Drive.'

Newer estates, red brick, no character. The houses were the same size as this place, bigger gardens, but worth about half the money. It was amazing how much people paid for a sea view. Louise had got in on the ground floor before anyone had heard of a property boom around here.

'The view of the Forth must be amazing,' Donna said, as if reading Surtsey's mind.

Out the kitchen window now, all they could see was a small scrap of grass and cobbles, the boatshed where they'd stowed the RIB.

'So tell me something I don't know about Donna Jones,' Surtsey said.

Donna looked down at the table and shrugged. 'There's not much to know.'

'There must be something, everyone has a story. What's yours?'

Donna shook her head. 'I used to be pretty good at ballet before I got big.'

'You're not big.'

'Too big for ballet.' Donna took a sip of her wine, licked her lips.

Surtsey tried to imagine Donna in a leotard. 'What else?'

'I can play drums,' Donna said.

'Really?'

'Learned as a kid.'

'Are you in a band?'

She shook her head. 'It's difficult getting the right people together. Plus it's hard to rehearse when you work shifts.'

Surtsey drank more wine. 'Do you want to work at St Columba's forever?'

Donna looked up, her mouth small. 'Maybe.'

'Doesn't it get depressing?'

'I like being able to help people in their moment of need.'

Surtsey thought about that. 'You're a better person than me, Donna.'

'I don't think so.'

'I'm sorry that I never knew you at school.'

'I always thought you were the coolest.'

Surtsey had her wine at her lips and spluttered. 'I think you have me confused with someone else.'

'You were different from the others. It didn't feel like you had to conform. You didn't give a shit about what anyone else thought.'

Surtsey raised her eyebrows. 'I'm not sure that trait has got me very far.'

Donna sipped. 'I remember you in the toilets at the end-of-year school disco once. I was with some other girls, Heather and her gang, they were all drunk on cider. They were talking about which boys they wanted to get off with, hassling me because I wasn't interested in that, saying I was a lezzer, all that rubbish. I was just shy and sober. You came out of a cubicle and just went off on one, going on about how nobody needed a boy to define them, how there was nothing wrong with being a lesbian anyway, how they were all narrow-minded idiots. You started going on about how you were going to get out of this shithole and do something with your life, unlike them. They all just stared like you were from another planet.'

'God, I spent the whole of school drunk, it seems. I don't remember that at all.'

'It was so cool, honestly.'

Surtsey smiled. 'Well I never got out of this shithole, did I?'

'Oh come on, you're doing a PhD, you'll be set for life in academia.'

Surtsey shook her head. 'I don't even know if that's what I want.'

'What else would you do?'

'I have no idea.'

Silence sat over them for a while but it didn't feel awkward, just as if they were old friends.

'Your mum talks about you all the time,' Donna said eventually.

'All bad, I presume.'

'She's so proud of you.'

'What do your parents think of your job?'

'They're both dead.'

'Oh shit, Donna, I'm sorry. I never knew.'

'There's no reason why you would know.'

Silence again.

'You want to know but you don't want to ask,' Donna said.

Surtsey put her hand out over the table. 'I don't want to upset you.'

Donna waved that away. 'It's fine, honestly. Mum drank a lot. I mean, a lot. I don't think she was ever happy at home with Dad, though she kept it away from me. They warned her but she kept drinking. Liver failure in the end, didn't take long.'

'I'm so sorry.'

'Dad got a new lease of life after she died, to be honest. Feels horrible to say, but he'd been shackled to her drinking for so long. It was amazing, he joined clubs and became sociable again, took up golf and Pilates. Then six months after Mum died I found him in bed one morning. Heart attack.'

Surtsey's hand was on Donna's now. 'I don't even know what to say.'

She wondered about her own mum dying, how she would cope. Would she keep on plugging away or spiral out of control?

'Hey, babes.'

Halima was leaning against the kitchen doorway as if she'd been there for a while. Her eyes went to Surtsey's hand on Donna's. Surtsey eased back in her chair, slid her hand away. She caught a flicker of a look in Donna's eye.

'Hey,' Surtsey said, between glugs of wine. 'This is Donna. Donna, this is Halima.'

'Hey,' Halima said.

'Hi.'

'Hal is doing a PhD too.' Surtsey turned to Halima. 'Donna works at the hospice up the road, looking after Mum.'

'And some other folk, I hope,' Halima said.

'We went to school together,' Surtsey said.

'Well, I was the year below,' Donna said.

Halima got a wine glass down from a cupboard and poured.

Donna scraped her chair as she stood up. 'Can I use your bathroom?'

'Upstairs, first on the left,' Surtsey said.

Halima watched as she left the room, her wine glass to her lips. She waited until Donna was upstairs then turned to Surtsey.

'Bringing new friends home now?'

'What's got into you?'

'She seems nice.'

Surtsey drank. 'She is. She's been a lot of help with Mum.'

'How come I've never met her before?'

'Because you've hardly ever been to St Columba's.'

'And how does Nurse Ratched feel about that?'

'Don't call her that. What's got into you?'

Halima folded her arms. 'Sorry, I just wasn't expecting company, it's been a fucker of a day.'

Surtsey looked out the window. 'Tell me about it.'

Halima stared at her. 'Did you have to lie to the police as well, yeah?'

Surtsey frowned for a second before remembering. 'Shit, Hal, sorry. How did it go?'

'Thanks for asking.'

'Christ, don't, I've had a crazy day. I forgot for a moment.'

'It's fine, I was just sweating in the police station lying for you, for reasons I don't understand, while you sat here playing happy families with your new buddy.'

'They interviewed you at the station?'

Halima's face softened. 'It was easier for me to go there on my way home, that's all.' Her wine glass was empty already so she refilled.

'How was it?'

Halima sipped. 'It was actually OK. They phoned me at the office after you did, I said I'd pop in. They took a statement. I said we were alone together at home that night, like we agreed. Said we just sat watching comedy and drinking. Which, like you said, is true.'

'Thanks, I really owe you.'

'Yes, you do.' Halima went to the doorway of the kitchen and looked up the stairs, checking to see if Donna was coming. 'I still don't understand why you can't tell them where you really were.'

'I told you I panicked,' Surtsey said. 'They were a pair of misogynist pricks. They thought I was a slut because I had two men on the go, I didn't want to add a third.'

Halima narrowed her eyes. 'Is that really it?'

'Yes.'

'There's nothing else you want to tell me?'

'Like what?'

'We're best friends, right?'

'Right.'

'I said I had you covered and I do. But if there's something else you want to tell me about this whole mess, now's the time.'

Footfall on the stairs, the squeak of a hand sliding down the banister.

'I best be going,' Donna said as she came into the kitchen. She hovered at the doorway looking at her wine glass, hardly touched on the table. 'Thanks for the drink.'

Surtsey got up, smiling. 'Thanks for today, Donna, I mean it.'

'It was nothing.'

'What happened today?' Halima said.

'Donna helped me take Mum to the Inch.'

'I was really just doing my job,' Donna said.

Surtsey began to walk her out. 'It was more than that, and you know it.'

Donna was at the door now. She looked back to the kitchen.

'Nice to meet you, Halima.'

Halima raised her glass. 'Cheers.'

Surtsey opened the door. Donna touched her arm, gave a little rub. 'You're being amazing for your mum.'

'I don't think so.'

'You really are,' Donna said. 'I wish I'd been as good a daughter as you.'

'Enough,' Surtsey said, not unkindly. 'Are you working tomorrow?'

Donna nodded. 'Early shift.'

'I'll pop in, not sure what time.'

'Bye, Surtsey.' Donna's hand was still on her arm.

'Bye.'

She watched Donna go down the path and through the gate, sodium lamplight making her dark hair glow. The way she walked wasn't confident, a self-consciousness about her body as she loped along the prom. She looked back and waved, and Surtsey was glad she'd stayed at the doorway to return the gesture.

She closed the door and went back to the kitchen where Halima was pouring the wine from Donna's glass into her own.

'Nursey seems nice.'

'If you're pissed off with me, fine,' Surtsey said. 'But don't take it out on her.'

'Whatever,' Halima said, heading upstairs. She dug out her hash pipe. 'I'm off for a bath.'

Surtsey went back to the kitchen and picked up her drink. She sipped it and looked out the back window at the boatshed. She heard the bath running upstairs and the bathroom door closing, music playing through the floor. After a moment the doorbell rang.

Surtsey headed for the door sipping her wine.

She opened it and her eyes widened. Alice stood there, hair a mess, eyes puffy, a raincoat over a summer dress. Cowering behind her legs were her daughters. Gracie was wide-eyed, staring at her mum, while the younger one, Belle, looked sleepy and confused.

'Shit,' Surtsey said. 'Alice.'

Alice's head was shaking, as if she was disagreeing with herself. 'Why did you come to my fucking house this morning?'

Surtsey's eyes shot to Gracie, who had her hand over her mouth. She was holding her little sister's hand with the other, and gave her a worried glance.

Surtsey smelled booze on Alice's breath.

'I know all about you,' Alice said, pointing. Her weight shifted, her hand wavering.

'Did you drive here drunk?' Surtsey said. 'With the girls in the car?'

Alice narrowed her eyes and focussed. 'Fuck you.'

Surtsey stepped forward and put an arm out towards her. Alice threw a hand wide and smacked the wine glass out of her hand. It smashed against the doorframe, showering them in shards, leaving Surtsey holding the stem and a ragged, curved star of glass. She noticed that the girls had bare feet.

'Careful,' she said to them. 'Step back.'

Alice put an arm around Gracie. 'Don't tell them what to do. They're nothing to do with you.'

'Then why did you bring them?' Surtsey said.

'Because I have no one to look after them. My husband is dead. I have no one else.'

Surtsey wanted to reach out but she kept still. The girls were both nervous now, Belle woken into focus by the breaking glass.

'Why don't you let me phone you a taxi,' Surtsey said.

Alice shook her head for a long time as if she couldn't believe what she was hearing.

'I think you did it,' she said.

'What?'

'You killed Tom.'

'Wait a minute,' Surtsey said.

'I spoke to the police,' Alice said. 'Told them what I know. Told them to look into you. They said you had an alibi, that you were here at home. Do you think I'm stupid? They might believe that shit but I know you had something to do with Tom on the Inch. I just know it.'

'I'm sorry, Alice,' Surtsey said. 'You're wrong.'

'If the police won't investigate you, I will, I'll find some evidence.'

Surtsey thought about the phone in her pocket. 'What do you mean?'

'I'm not going to leave this,' Alice said. Her nose was running, voice trembling. 'I'm going to make you pay.'

'Mum,' Gracie said. 'Please.'

'It's OK, darling,' Alice said. 'I'm just talking to this...'

She couldn't find the right word.

Surtsey looked at the cowering girls, thought about Tom.

'You should leave,' she said, the broken glass still in her hand. 'Please don't drive in this state.'

Alice shook her head, teeth tight. She pushed her thumbs into her fists, squeezing, barely containing her rage.

'Don't tell me what to do,' she said. 'Do you understand?'

'Think of the girls,' Surtsey said.

Alice looked like she'd been punched. 'I think of them every second of every day. Everything I do, every fucking thing, is for them. And now I have to do it alone. You have no idea what that's like. I hope you do, some day, I hope you have everything taken away from you.'

Surtsey thought of her mum up the road, of Tom on the black sand.

'What do you mean?'

Alice spoke softly. 'I'm going to destroy you like you've destroyed me.'

'That sounds like a threat.'

'It is, believe me.'

'Please leave.'

'You'll be sorry.' Alice released her fists and stretched her fingers. 'You're going to be sorry you ever set eyes on my husband.'

She grabbed the girls by the shoulders and turned them away, then strode down the path, the girls scrambling after her into the night.

25

Too much grass, red wine and guilt. Surtsey lay on her bed and tried to focus. She looked at her bedside lamp but it kept drifting across her vision, trailing floaters. She closed her eyes and saw Tom, the gentle collapse of his skull. She imagined lifting a rock and making that dent, destroying the structure of his face. She knew the power of the earth, the weight of stone. She understood that. How thin the layer of each person was, just hair, skin, sinew, muscle, bone. When the barrier between you and the outside world was broken and your insides were spilling out onto the sand you became part of the world. You returned to the earth, finally home, your atoms mixing with the universe again, interconnected in a way you could never be whilst alive.

Shit, that grass was strong. She was thirsty.

She blinked heavily, then eased herself up like an old woman. Put her hands in front of her like a mummy from an old movie, touched the wall then the door, then went to the bathroom and filled a glass with water. The feel of it in her throat was electrifying. She drank and refilled then wobbled back to her room and thumped the pint glass on the bedside table, fell back onto the bed.

She tried to look at the poster of the Inch on her wall. Steam billowing into the sky from the blue-green water, lava flow glowing, throbbing against the black rock, a shard of lightning connecting the earth to the sky. She thought of something she'd seen in a documentary. When a bolt of lightning strikes from above, all these little tracers spark up from dozens of points across the land in the first few microseconds, each of them desperate to connect with the motherbolt. They raise their ionised hands to heaven waiting for the rapture, hoping to be the chosen one, to be connected and lifted to the sky.

She heard a ping and looked around the room.

She felt a charge move through her like she was one of those streamers reaching out to the lightning, waiting for the bolt.

She pulled Tom's phone out of her pocket and looked at the screen:

Do you feel guilty?

She blinked. Blinked again. Started typing slowly:

I've done nothing wrong.

The phone felt hot in her hand as if it was faulty. It pinged:

That's not what the police think.

She dropped it on the bed and stared at it. Picked it up and typed:

I'm going to tell the police about you. Give them this phone.

For a second she imagined again that it was the Inch itself sending the messages. The island knew her innermost fears and secrets, knew her inside out, saw everything she did there. She slapped herself in the face trying to clear her mind.

She stared again at the messages, the letters drifting in her stoned vision, left to right like she'd been on a roundabout.

The phone pinged again.

She closed her eyes, needed a moment before reading. She concentrated on her lungs expanding and contracting, interacting with the atmosphere at a microscopic level.

Opened her eyes:

No you won't. They wouldn't believe you anyway.

'I didn't kill him,' she said.

Her voice didn't sound convincing.

Ping:

Returning to the crime scene wasn't smart.

Surtsey rubbed at the skin beneath her eyes. Pushed at the sockets until her focus blurred. Felt tears come.

She looked around the room then touched the screen, slow, fingers clumsy:

Who are you?

Send.

She sat looking at the screen waiting for an answer, but no answer came.

26

She was an ancient god made of stone, held captive in the core of the earth. Slowly the magma melted her chains until she broke free, swimming in the molten rock, upwards towards the surface, faster and faster, the pressure around her lessening until she burst into water then open air, fists held high, lava and rock and steam surrounding her as she soared into the atmosphere and gazed down on the planet from space, marvelling that only minutes before it had been her prison.

A ringing.

She bumped out of sleep, head in a fug, the raw rasp of grass sticking in her throat and mouth.

Phone. It was a ring not a ping, a call not a message.

She clambered for Tom's phone, pulled it from under the pillow. Nothing. She stared at it, the ringing still in her ears.

Not Tom's phone. Hers.

She found it on the floor next to the bed.

St Columba's.

They never usually called. In fact, she couldn't think of a time they'd ever called her.

Her stomach slumped and her skin prickled.

She didn't answer straight away.

Six rings, seven.

Ten.

She pressed the button.

'Hello?'

'Hello, is this Ms Mackenzie?'

The formality confirmed it.

'Yes.'

'This is Deborah Steel, the registered nurse at St Columba's Hospice. I'm afraid I have some bad news.'

'Yes.'

'I'm sorry but your mother Louise passed away in the night.'

'Yes.'

Like she couldn't say anything else, like she was stuck on 'yes' for the rest of her life.

'It was peaceful,' the nurse said. 'In her sleep. I'm so sorry.'

Surtsey looked at the poster on her wall, lightning delivering hundreds of amps, shooting life into the Inch. She thought about yesterday with her mum, touching the sand, breathing the air.

'Is there someone there with you?' the nurse said.

Surtsey had forgotten the nurse was still there and jumped at the sound of her voice. She thought about the question, looked at her bedroom door. Halima down the hall, if she wasn't up and out already. Iona too. Shit.

'Yes,' she said. It seemed easiest. Just go along with all this, follow protocol. Deliver her lines as best she could, hope that everyone was convinced she was still human, still breathing.

'I'm afraid I have to ask you a couple of questions, Ms Mackenzie.'

'Surtsey.'

'Pardon?'

'It's my name.'

'Surtsey, yes. Is it OK if I ask you a few things?'

'Sure.' Surtsey took the phone away from her ear for a second and stared at it. The little smudged area at the top of the screen where her ear had been pressed. The red button to end the call. She put it on speaker to feel less intimate, less connected.

'Wait a minute,' she said. 'I have some questions first. Is that OK?'

'Of course.'

Surtsey tried to remember the nurse's name but it was already gone.

'How did it happen?' she said.

A pause while Surtsey stared at the screen.

'As I said, your mother passed away peacefully in the night.'

'From what?'

'I'm sorry?'

'What did she die of?'

'Surtsey, Louise had terminal cancer. You know that.'

'Yes, but what specifically killed her?'

'The cancer killed her.'

'I was with her yesterday. She was fine.' Surtsey pictured her mum on the boat, spray in her hair and wind whipping around them both.

'That's often the case in my experience,' the nurse said. 'Clients frequently perk up before the end.'

'It wasn't like that.'

'I understand it's hard to accept,' the nurse said. 'I'm so sorry.'

'I can accept it,' Surtsey said. 'It's just...'

Silence.

Eventually Surtsey spoke, as much to herself as into the phone. 'Couldn't you have kept her alive a little longer?'

'It was her time,' the nurse said.

'How do you know it was peaceful?' Surtsey said.

'Sorry?'

'You said she died peacefully in her sleep. How do you know? How do you know she wasn't writhing in agony for hours while your staff were pissing around on Facebook or reading *Hello* magazine?'

'She was asleep,' the nurse said, 'and she didn't wake up. And anyway, she had a DNR order in her paperwork.'

'What?'

'Do Not Resuscitate. We discussed it when she first came. She didn't mention it to you?'

She had done, Surtsey remembered, but it seemed so far away, a theoretical discussion with no relevance to her mum actually fucking dying.

The nurse spoke again. 'So even if someone had been with her, we couldn't have done anything. Legally, I mean.'

'Did you see her yesterday?'

'I'm sorry?'

'You personally, did you see my mum yesterday?'

Surtsey heard a sigh down the phone. What must it be like to give people this information all day long? To be the one who steps into people's lives and gives them the worst news imaginable? The harbinger of death, a real-life grim reaper.

'I spoke to Louise at teatime,' the nurse said.

'And did she seem to you, as a professional, like someone about to die?'

'It's not like that. You never know.'

'So what's the point of all the nursing training, if you can't tell when someone is going to die?'

Here eyes were wet with tears, dripping onto the phone screen. She didn't wipe them away, worried she might end the call by accident, end this final connection with her mum. If they could just keep talking, maybe Louise wasn't really dead. A clerical error, someone typed the wrong name into the computer, it happened all the time.

'I'm sorry, but I do have to ask a couple of questions,' the nurse said. Diplomatic, unprovokable. What must that be like?

'OK.'

'Firstly, did your mother have an end-of-life plan?'

'What?'

'A plan for what to do when this happens. We have no note of one in our records. Normally if a client has one we would have a copy.'

Client. Louise Mackenzie, aged forty-six, just another fucking client. But then how else would you deal with it if you had to do it every day? All these dead and dying weren't your relatives, or you would go insane with grief and stress.

Surtsey looked at her bedside table hoping to see Hal's hash pipe. She saw a glass of water and lunged for it, gulping it down, cold in her throat. She gasped as she finished it.

'Ms Mackenzie?'

'I don't know about a plan. I don't have a plan.'

'Then you'll need to organise a funeral director to come and collect your mum.'

'You mean her body.'

'Yes. If you don't have a funeral director in mind I can recommend a local one.'

'Who has a funeral director in mind?'

Silence.

Surtsey sighed. 'I'm sorry, a recommendation would be good. But don't we need to get the coroner or whatever first?'

'When death isn't suspicious there's no need to contact the coroner or police. I'm registered to sign the death certificate and a funeral director takes care of the deceased's body after that.'

'What about cause of death?'

'We know the cause of death,' the nurse said. 'As we have already discussed.'

'So that's it? Can I at least see her?'

'Of course,' the nurse said. 'That was my next question. Would you like to see her here as she is, or later after the funeral director has prepared her?'

'Prepared her how?'

'It's rather delicate.'

'Try me.'

'Bodies decompose and that process starts immediately. Your mother is fine right now, but we're required by law to have her taken care of as soon as possible. If you want to come in and see her, it's best to do it sooner rather than later.'

Surtsey pictured Iona sprawled across her bed, in a thick, booze-sodden sleep, oblivious to this wrecking ball through their lives.

'OK,' she said eventually. 'I'll be round to see her as soon as possible.'

27

She stood outside Iona's room staring at the door. The whitewash was peeling at the edges, the wood scuffed and chipped around the door handle. Who would repaint the door when it needed done? Surtsey ran a finger over one dent around head height, remembered throwing a trainer at her sister only to have the door slammed in the way. She touched the mark now, tried to remember what the trainer was like. Four large wooden letters were stuck to Iona's door across the middle, fairy lights set into them, but the batteries had run out on the final 'A', leaving 'ION'. A charged particle, quick to react. Surtsey tried to think of a joke about that.

She knocked. 'Iona?'

Knocked again.

Nothing.

She pushed the door open. The place was a midden, stale booze and dope and sweat in the air.

Iona was out for the count, hair over her face, her arm flung over a naked guy on top of the bedclothes. His head was turned away but Surtsey could see a grey beard, a sinewy, weathered body, tight buttocks and a fat cock. Against his dark skin, Iona looked pale and beautiful.

'Iona,' Surtsey said.

Iona came to the surface slowly.

'What time is it?'

'We need to talk.'

'Fuck off.' Iona put an arm across her face, covering her eyes.

Surtsey sighed. This was never going to come again, this moment when her sister didn't know. Once Surtsey spoke, it was over.

'Mum died, Iona.'

She expected protestation, disbelief, but maybe something in her voice got across.

Iona sat up, not bothering to cover herself. 'What?'

'The hospice just called.'

'What happened?'

'She died in her sleep last night. It's over.'

Iona rubbed her head. 'No, that's not right.'

'I'm afraid so.'

'But you saw her yesterday.'

Surtsey stood feeling awkward, trying not to look at the naked man still asleep.

Iona breathed deeply. 'This is just...'

'Put something on and come downstairs.'

'Fuck, this isn't happening.'

'I'm sorry.'

A look of clarity on Iona's face when she heard that. She looked at Surtsey, something terrible in her eyes.

'Me too,' she said.

The guy in bed rolled over, still sleeping, and Surtsey recognised him without his glasses. Bastian.

'What the fuck?' she said.

She stared at him for a moment, then looked at Iona.

'You're fucking this guy?'

'So what?'

'He's the leader of those New Thule morons.'

Iona frowned. 'So what?'

Surtsey shoved at Bastian's chest, hard. 'Hey.'

He stirred and took a second to come to.

Surtsey turned to her sister. 'I honestly can't fucking believe you.'

She spoke to Bastian, who was putting his glasses on.

'You get the fuck out of my house,' she said. 'And stay away from my little sister.'

28

They scurried along the prom, sharp easterly taking the edge off the thin sunshine. A woman threw a ball along the shoreline for her Labrador, some old guy doing tai chi facing out to sea. The Inch had a wreath of white cloud around its base, like bubbles in a bath. The sun would burn that off or the wind would blow it away, and the island would soon be exposed.

Iona ran her hands through her hair, fluffing it backwards and forwards.

Surtsey pictured her sister underneath Bastian, grunting and groaning as he thrust away, then they both climaxed, but the faces got mixed up and it was her and Tom going at it on the Inch. She remembered Tom's phone, the messages last night. They seemed irrelevant now.

Iona lagged behind, out of breath. Surtsey concentrated on the air in and out of her lungs.

Iona stopped.

'Come on,' Surtsey said.

A defiant look. 'Let's just take a fucking minute, shall we?'

'I said we'd be there as soon as possible.'

'She's dead.'

'So?'

'What's the rush? She's not going anywhere.'

Surtsey breathed deeply and looked out to sea. She couldn't see Berwick Law in this visibility or the Paps of Fife across the water. She could just make out an oil tanker smudging the horizon.

'She's going off,' she said.

'What?'

'The nurse told me. They need to get her refrigerated.'

'Christ.' Iona put a hand out.

Surtsey realised she was crying, shoulders shaking, heaving breath, snot from her nose right there on the prom as a woman went past pushing a double buggy. She imagined Louise walking along the prom with Surtsey and Iona at that age, coping with the handful, happy in the moment, enjoying the sunshine and the wind and the fact that they were all alive and healthy and the only concern was when they would need a sleep or a nappy change, if they might throw a tantrum over not getting a sweetie or having to eat some fruit, or something even more stupid like not having the right shoes on, the red ones not the pink ones, despite the fact the pink ones didn't fit any more, hurt her feet, gave her blisters and pinched at her toes.

She felt her sister's arms around her and let herself be held.

'I'm getting snot on your shoulder,' she said eventually, laughing through it.

'I've had worse. Some guy puked on my shoes last night at closing time.'

Surtsey pulled back and looked in Iona's eyes.

'What are we going to do now?'

'I don't know,' Iona said. 'Just keep going, I guess.'

Surtsey swallowed hard, wiped at her eyes and nose.

'Yeah,' she said. 'Maybe that's all there is to it.'

29

They spoke to Effie at reception who came round and gave both girls a hug, then took them in a different direction to Louise's bedroom.

'Where are we going?' Surtsey said.

'They moved her,' Effie said.

'Why?'

'It's just what they do.'

They turned left then went through a passageway to the back of the building. Effie stopped at a door.

'Your mum's in here,' she said, touching Surtsey's arm. 'Take as long as you need.'

She left them to it. Surtsey watched her walk away.

'Why did they move her?' Iona said. 'Do they need the bed already?'

'Don't.'

'Maybe they don't want to scare the other inmates, avoid the Grim Reaper's touch.'

'Iona, please.'

The air was colder here, overhead vents leaking air.

Surtsey stared at the ceiling grid for a moment.

'Are you ready?' she said.

'Fuck no.'

Surtsey touched Iona's face. She could still smell the vodka on her breath, her hair greasy at the roots. Last night's make-up was smudged in the corners of her eyes.

Surtsey pushed the door open. The air was colder in here, two lamps casting delicate light on to the ceiling. Louise was neatly tucked into a bed in the middle of the room, three cheaply upholstered chairs alongside.

It was obvious straight away she was gone. The skin of her face was waxy and pale, a grey tinge to the lips.

Surtsey struggled to swallow.

With just her head and arms showing, Louise looked like she was being consumed by the bed, sucked down into a soft underworld of sheets and pillows.

There was nothing after this, no heaven or hell, no afterlife, just silence. Louise had believed that with all her heart and Surtsey did too. Religion was false comfort in the face of oblivion, a respite against our own insignificance. But being free from that was comforting in its own way. If you weren't waiting for the afterlife you could concentrate on living.

Did her mum do that? Do any of us? It's handy for eulogies, a beautiful lie, but really we all just stumble along from one day to the next without dying or harming others, without too much embarrassment or awkwardness, without confronting anything too shocking. Something from a play at school came to her. 'I can't go on, I'll go on'.

Her mum didn't look happy or sad or relieved or anything. Just dead. Gone.

Iona touched her mum's hand and jerked away.

'Christ, she's cold.'

'What did you expect?'

'It's just freaky, that's all.'

Surtsey reached out and placed the back of her fingers against her mum's hand. She moved her hand to Louise's cheek.

They stood in silence.

Goosebumps rose on Surtsey's arms from the air con. Of course, keeping the body cool to reduce decomposition. So matter of fact, the logistics of death.

'Do you want to say anything?' Surtsey said eventually.

'Like what?'

Surtsey shrugged. She had no clue how to do this. 'I don't know.'

She turned to the body, took the cold hand in hers, gripped it. She felt her sister staring at her as she took a deep breath and spoke.

'What do we do now, Mum?' She slackened her grip, touched the bedsheets then spoke again, this time under her breath. 'What do we do now?'

*

They scuffed over the floor tiles, Iona trailing a finger along the wall. Surtsey wanted this to mean something, to connect with her sister. But we can't ever know someone else's mind, we can't even guess what others are thinking. We certainly can't make them feel what we want them to.

She wondered what Louise had thought of them. Did she think she'd been a success as a mother?

Effie was out of her seat before they reached reception, her head tilted in sympathy.

'You girls OK?'

Iona shook her head, making it clear the question was meaningless.

'Fine, thanks,' Surtsey said.

'Nurse Steel says she's sorry she couldn't be here,' Effie said.

Surtsey had to think hard who that was. The woman on the phone.

'She'll be in touch about all the paperwork,' Effie said.

'Paperwork?' Iona said, as if Effie had mentioned aliens.

'Just a few forms, nothing to worry about.'

'Thanks for everything, Effie,' Surtsey said.

Effie smiled and went back behind the reception desk, then held up a rucksack. It was Louise's, a sturdy hillwalking thing she used for fieldwork for years. They'd used it to bring Louise's belongings when she first came here. So here it was again, now they were leaving.

'All her stuff's in there,' Effie said. She lowered her voice. 'I made sure they washed the clothes she was in.'

Iona stared at her. 'Why?'

Effie looked awkward. 'It's just better.'

The body soiled itself, Surtsey realised, once the heart gave up.

'Thanks.'

She lifted the rucksack onto her shoulder, enjoyed the weight of it on her back, and headed for the door with Iona.

'You girls take care,' Effie said as the door closed behind them.

'Fancy a drink?' Iona said.

30

Surtsey sat on the wall outside the Espy staring at the sea. The rowing club were out again, half a dozen of them dipping their oars in unison, heading east towards Fisherrow in Musselburgh. She pictured the water spraying on their hunched over backs, the tang of the air in their nostrils. She wanted to be out there, not anchored to the earth. Further along the beach a couple of swimmers in wetsuits were splashing out to the marker buoys. Surtsey tried to imagine the shock of the cold water on her skin, the ache in her limbs.

Iona appeared beside her waving a bottle of tequila. 'Come on.'

She jumped down onto the sand and strode towards the water.

'Did you just lift that from the pub?' Surtsey said, wiping the sand from her bum and following.

'They won't miss it.'

'They will.'

Iona broke the seal on the bottle. 'So what?'

They walked alongside the old groyne, barnacles on the wrinkled wood, pools of water where the support struts disappeared into the sand. Surtsey saw a crab scuttling into the shadows, and wondered what other life lurked down there.

The tide was halfway in, the end of the groyne underwater. They stopped at the edge of the dry sand and plonked themselves down. Iona had already taken a couple of swigs from the bottle. She wiped the top on her sleeve and passed it to Surtsey who drank, screwed her eyes shut as the burn spread from her chest like she'd been struck by lightning.

'Christ,' she said. 'That's the good stuff. They're definitely going to miss that.'

She passed it back.

Out at sea the rowers were struggling into a headwind while the swimmers had rounded the buoy and were heading west to the next marker.

'Why did you get the call?' Iona said.

'What?'

'Why did the hospice phone you?'

'I'm the emergency contact.'

'Who decided that?'

'Mum.'

'That sounds about right.'

'What does that mean?'

'You know.' Iona gulped tequila like water.

'Come on, don't do this now.'

Iona passed the bottle. 'Don't do what?'

Surtsey took it and drank. 'Please.'

Iona sighed. The wind threw a skim of grains scurrying over the surface of the sand. Two oystercatchers were snooping about the little craters left by razor clams under the surface. Further along, a toddler in just a nappy was challenging the incoming waves, slapping forward over the wet sand as the tide receded, giggling and running back to her mum as the water came rushing in again. Chase me, chase me.

Surtsey tried to remember being that age. She must've done the same thing as a wee kid but she couldn't remember. She'd seen plenty of pictures, beach photos of the three of them having a picnic or barbecue, building terrible sandcastles that fell apart, palming a beach ball to each other. She wondered if she remembered these things or if she had constructed memories from the photographs.

The toddler fell to her knees, got straight up, unconcerned about her sandy legs. Time compressed to nothing in Surtsey's mind, in the blink of an eye from a kid playing in the sand to a woman with no mother.

Iona took the bottle from her and drank.

'What was the last thing you said to her?' she said.

Surtsey blew out air, felt heartburn from the tequila.

'I can't remember.'

'Try harder,' Iona said.

'Why does it matter?'

'It's important.'

Surtsey shook her head. 'You want some profound sign-off, an epiphany, is that it?'

'What's wrong with that?'

'It's bullshit,' Surtsey said. 'Arguing about whether a window should be open or not, or the strength of the tea in a café, that's life. That's just as important as last words, or life advice or whatever you think you need.'

'So you don't remember?'

Surtsey sighed. 'Probably just "goodbye" or "sleep well" or "see you tomorrow".'

The last words stuck in her throat as she took the bottle.

Iona closed her eyes and touched her forehead. 'I called her a bitch.'

'What?'

She shook her head. 'She was having a go at me about the pub job. Wanted me to fulfil my potential.' Her voice made quote marks around the phrase.

'She's got a point.'

'She was using her illness, guilt-tripping me. I told her to shut the fuck up.'

Surtsey handed the bottle back. They sat in silence for a moment. 'That's my point. It doesn't matter what we said or what she said. She was our mum, she loved us, we loved her. That's it.'

The rowing club were almost out of sight to the east, just a blip on the water. Closer by, the swimmers were trudging out of the shallows like monsters from the deep, walking heavily. The toddler had found a stick and was tracing shapes in the sand, a slice of apple in her other hand. Her mum was watching closely.

Surtsey looked at her sister. 'How the hell did you end up fucking that Bastian guy?'

Iona shrugged. 'How does anyone end up fucking anyone? He came into the pub, we got talking, he was nice.'

'He's in his forties.'

Iona laughed. 'Hello? Tom?'

Surtsey sighed. 'He's bad news.'

'How do you mean?'

Surtsey thought about the Inch, all the people connected with it in some way.

'I'm not sure, he just is.'

'Sur, he's just a fucking guy,' Iona said. 'They're ten a penny. It doesn't mean anything.'

She took a hit of tequila and winced.

'Do you think Mum knew?' she said.

'What?'

'When you saw her yesterday. How was she?'

Surtsey considered the question for a long moment. Pictured Louise on the Inch letting the sand run through her fingers. 'She was on good form. Happy to be out on the water, even happier on the island.'

'Was it her idea to go out?'

Surtsey tried to remember. 'Yeah.'

'Maybe she knew she was going to die.'

'We all knew she was going to die. She had cancer.'

'You know what I mean,' Iona said. 'In the night.'

'I don't know.'

Iona passed the bottle back. It was half empty already. At some point they would have to stop and sober up.

Surtsey swigged and smacked her lips, getting a taste for it. 'She seemed so lively yesterday. More energy.'

'She knew.'

'You weren't there.'

Iona stared at her, took the bottle. 'Rub it in, why don't you?'

'Sorry.'

'It's typical you would have a great last day with her out on the ocean, mother and daughter sharing a final moment while I was serving lager to pot-bellied arseholes, doing the shit job she wanted me to quit.'

She waved the bottle over her shoulder at the pub back on the prom. A spurt of tequila left the bottle and made a splat on the sand.

'Don't,' Surtsey said.

She reached out to touch her sister's hand but Iona misinterpreted and handed her the bottle.

'Why not?' Iona said. 'It doesn't matter now.'

Silence for a while between them before Iona spoke again.

'Nothing matters now.'

31

When they got home, Iona phoned the Espy to say she was sick. They didn't believe her, not least because she'd been in earlier to liberate the tequila, but she hung up before she could get a bollocking. She drank a pint of water then took the dregs of the tequila to bed. Surtsey watched her slouch up the stairs and wondered if she would sleep, if either of them would ever sleep again.

Halima wasn't around, Surtsey presumed she'd gone into the office. Surtsey would have to tell her about Louise, and she suddenly felt the burden of that. Halima had felt awkward about moving in when Louise moved out; imagine taking your best friend's mum's bedroom in a shared house.

Surtsey took her mum's rucksack to the living room, opened it and began lifting things out. Some nightclothes at the top, cleaned and neatly folded. Then a toilet bag full of nondescript items – toothbrush, sponge, moisturisers and the like. Louise had never been fussy about her appearance – no strict regimen of creams or make-up, just throw together whatever felt right and get out the door. That had continued in the hospice, even less reason to care when you weren't going to be around forever.

Underneath the toilet bag were some books on volcanology and copies of *New Scientist*. Before the diagnosis Louise read a lot of fiction, mostly detective stories, but she reverted to non-fiction once she had cancer, said she didn't want to waste time in made-up worlds. She kept up on developments in geophysics, interested in new analysis techniques and theories about seismic disturbance.

Near the bottom of the rucksack Surtsey pulled out some photographs, a Boots packet stuffed with fading images of the three of them through the years. Surtsey felt sick as she flicked through them, a lifetime in thirty-seven photos. Nothing amazing, just snaps on birthdays, Iona blowing out six candles, a beach shot with a picnic of sandwiches and lemon drizzle cake. It was the only thing Louise could bake from scratch and Surtsey craved it now.

She felt something under her feet, another tremor. Christ, they were happening all the time now. This was a light one, more a shimmer of the air than anything substantial, but still tangible in her body. She gripped a photograph, smudging the edge. It was over in a few seconds, a change in air pressure from the windows moving in their frames, then that was it. She looked up at the ceiling and wondered if Iona was awake to feel it.

She remembered something she'd read about how early humans had prayed to forces of nature – earthquakes, volcanoes, lightning storms – any displays of power inducing awe in primitive minds. That power highlighted our own insignificance, made us humble. And it went further back to apes, she'd seen a documentary about bonobos in Africa demonstrating similar behaviour. The presenter said it was because social groups got bigger and needed something to replace the conventional alpha animal. What better replacement than God in the shape of the trembling earth, a tidal wave, molten rock spewing from the ground? It was the need to impose order on chaos, the urge for a higher power to blame, a god to appease. But what happened when you did everything in your power to appease them, then they still destroyed you? What happened when your god deserted you? Your mum can die of cancer days after your lover is murdered, why not? There's no reason to any of it.

Surtsey held a pair of red heels that she'd pulled from the bag. She couldn't remember Louise wearing them since she went to St Columba's, though she'd loved them and worn them often beforehand. Her life had become reduced, that was the truth. Why add more discomfort in the form of heels when you were fighting against the pain of your body destroying itself?

Louise had raged about the language of cancer, the combative imagery of 'fighting' and 'beating' it. Cancer was part of you, it *was* you, so fighting cancer meant fighting yourself. How could you win that battle? It was too simplistic and the way cancer charities exploited it left a bad taste. Surtsey had never considered it until her mum was diagnosed. Louise ranted to the consultant when he wheeled out the tired old lines. There had to be a better metaphor, or maybe metaphors weren't the answer. You just had to live with it until you couldn't any more.

There was a tiny ripple under Surtsey's feet, a short aftershock, as if the house was breathing. Then just the clock on the mantelpiece with its thin tick, the burr of bike wheels as a cyclist passed outside.

The rucksack was almost empty now. Surtsey stuck her hand in and pulled out the last item, an envelope. Louise's elegant writing on the front: *To My Girls*. She weighed it in her hand for a moment, listened to the clock ticking, then opened it.

Surtsey & Iona,

I'm sorry I can't be with you any more, but my time was up. At least I got to see you both grow into beautiful, smart, independent women. Being a parent is hard, you spend your whole life wondering what you did wrong, what you could've done better, worrying that you're fucking up your kids for life with your own hang-ups. But looking at you two now, I think maybe I didn't fuck up too badly.

I know it's hard now, but try to celebrate life, for me. Try to live life to the fullest, take chances, follow your hearts. I know that's a terrible cliché, but it's true, you really have to seize every moment. I don't doubt that you'll both have amazing full lives and incredible experiences like I did, and that thought fills my heart with joy.

In one sense, it wasn't easy bringing you two up myself, but in fact you both made it so easy. Of course you were both total pains at times, from toddlers to teenagers, but I wouldn't swap a single second of it. Please know that you made my life worth living from beginning to end.

But it was my decision to raise you on my own. I always told you that your father left us when you were little, but that's not exactly true.

Surtsey broke off reading to wipe tears from her eyes and take a breath. She heard some girls laughing outside on the prom and thought about what Louise wrote. She had never hidden from her and Iona who their dad was, a professor of climate science at the University of Canterbury in Christchurch called Andrew Ford. He left before Iona was born, Louise claiming it just wasn't working out. These days he had his own family on the other side of the world, and Surtsey and her sister got birthday cards and nothing else. Surtsey realised she would have to tell him about Louise too. She sniffed and turned back to the letter.

Andrew and I did split up, that much is true. But it was because of me. I had an affair with a colleague. Andrew found out. It was pretty simple, really, I was pregnant, and Andrew and I hadn't been intimate for a while. Even then, he was willing to try to make things work, but I was so guilty and ashamed, I couldn't. I had the affair because I wasn't in love with Andrew any more, and I couldn't live a life pretending that I was. That's the worst thing you can do, girls, live a lie.

The colleague was Tom Lawrie. He's Iona's father, not Andrew.

Surtsey's hands were shaking as she gripped the edge of the paper. She tried to swallow but couldn't seem to do it. She closed her eyes and tried to breathe, her exhale was shaky and erratic. She touched her face with her hand, her whole body trembling. Christ almighty. She opened her eyes and forced herself to read the rest of the letter.

I'm sorry I never told you, that was stupid and selfish of me. But Tom was with someone, is happily married to her now, and they have a family. I didn't want to destroy that. Maybe now, now that so much dust has settled, Iona, you can have some kind of relationship with your dad, I don't know. I hope so.

Surtsey checked the letter for a date. Nothing. Written before everything that had happened. Fuck.

I'm so sorry to tell you this, and I'm so ashamed that I kept this a secret. It has eaten away at me all these years, my one regret in life. But once the initial decision was made, it became harder and harder to tell you the truth. Secrets can kill you, girls, try to live your life without them, and you will be much happier.

I love you both so much more than I can put into words. I'm so sorry that I'm not with you any more, but please live with me in your hearts.

Love, love, love Louise xx

Surtsey stared at the last words through blurry eyes, her whole body shaking as if there was another quake. She thought about Louise, and Tom, and Iona, and ran to the kitchen sink and was sick into the basin, retching until there was nothing left, the burn in her throat, her eyes watering. She rinsed her mouth and spat, then stared at the ceiling.

She went back to the living room, picked up the letter, and dragged her weary legs upstairs. She stood looking outside Iona's door, then let her head rest on it for a moment.

She knocked, and her heart sank when Iona replied.

'Come in.'

She felt like she was in a nightmare, unable to control her own body, forced to move forwards into situations she couldn't handle.

Iona was on the bed on her phone, the reek of tequila everywhere. She didn't look up. Surtsey held up the letter.

'You need to read this.'

Iona glanced up and pressed her mouth into a line.

'What is it?'

'It's from Mum.'

Iona lowered her phone and something registered from seeing the look on Surtsey's face. She took the letter and squinted at it, started reading, the tip of her tongue poking out the side of her mouth in concentration.

Surtsey stood still, watching. Iona just read. It seemed to take forever.

She looked up once, shared a look with Surtsey, returned to the letter. She shook her head, mumbling 'no, no, no' under her breath like a mantra. She put a hand out on the bed, her fingers gripping the covers, her head still shaking, her eyes beginning to water up. Eventually she looked up.

'Holy fuck.'

Surtsey gulped. 'Yeah.'

'Holy fucking fuck.' She returned to the letter, read to the end, breathed deeply.

Silence for a long time.

Iona looked out the window, her chest rising and falling, staring at nothing. Some sparrows on a telephone line, a seagull scratching across a neighbour's roof.

'So,' she said eventually. 'My mum and dad have both died this week. Good times.'

'I'm so sorry,' Surtsey said.

'And you were...' Iona raised her eyebrows at how ridiculous it all was.

'I know.'

Iona laughed. 'Old enough to be your father, right?'

'Don't.'

Iona picked up the tequila bottle from the floor and lifted it to her lips but it was empty. She dropped it and burst out crying, just sat there hunched over on her bed, her shoulders shaking, sobbing, her hands to her face.

Surtsey sat on the bed and put her arms around her, just shushed and rocked her, like when they were little and she'd grazed her knee on the prom or been stung by a jellyfish on the sand.

They sat like that for a long time in each other's arms, not speaking. There was nothing to say.

32

The doorbell.

Surtsey came to with a start. She was lying on top of the covers on Iona's bed, spooning her sister. She didn't know how long she'd slept. The letter was on the floor next to the tequila bottle. She blinked a few times, shook her head, tried to get her shit together.

The doorbell again.

Surtsey sat up slowly and placed her feet on the floor. Iona hadn't moved an inch, was out cold. Surtsey stood up and walked down the stairs, dreading whoever was on the other side of the door. She put her hand on the snib, breathed, then opened it.

'I'm so sorry,' Donna said. 'About your mum.'

Tears came up and out of Surtsey in a flood, a hot rush she couldn't quell, gasping and sobbing, reaching for Donna and pulling her into the house, burying her face in the woman's shoulder, clutching at her back in a hug, swaying on her feet as if another aftershock was throbbing through them both.

They stood in the hallway with the front door open, Surtsey immersed in the smell and feel of the other woman, not thinking anything for as long as she could manage. Eventually she became aware of passers-by on the prom, an elderly couple, one pushing the other in a wheelchair, two young women in training gear walking fast and gossiping, a dad with a baby in a harness on his chest.

She pulled back from Donna, her fresh scent lingering in her nose.

'I'm sorry,' she said.

'Don't be.'

Surtsey reached for the door and shut it.

'How are you doing?' Donna said.

'Not great.'

'I can't imagine.'

Surtsey showed Donna through to the kitchen. 'Can I get you anything?'

Donna frowned. 'Sit down, I'll get the kettle on.'

Surtsey smiled and wiped her nose with a tissue, did the same with her tears on her sleeve. She leaned against the small table, not wanting to sit down in case she never got back up. She thought for a moment.

'Was it you who found her?'

Donna shook her head. 'One of the night shift, just before I came on this morning.'

'They didn't call me straight away?'

'The charge nurse has to verify the death before informing next of kin.'

'Right.'

'I wanted to call you, but I wasn't allowed.'

She got mugs from hooks, opened a cupboard and threw teabags into them. Her sense of calm reminded Surtsey of her mum, but then everything made her think of Louise at the moment. Donna finished making tea then handed one to Surtsey.

'Are you sure you don't want to sit down?'

'I'm fine.'

Donna made a show of looking round the kitchen. 'Where are your housemates?'

Surtsey shook her head. 'Halima's at the office, Iona's upstairs sleeping it off. She came with me to the hospice this morning. The nurse said we had to do it straight away.'

'That's normal.'

Surtsey sipped her tea. 'Did you see her?'

Donna nodded. 'I hope you don't mind, I popped in after the night-shift nurse told me. I wanted to say goodbye.'

'That's nice, you and her were close.'

Donna looked around the room again. Surtsey realised it was a nervous gesture.

'What is it?' Surtsey said.

Donna shook her head. 'I don't know if I should bring it up.'

'Well, you have to now.'

Donna took a big drink of tea, eyes down. She took something from her pocket, put it down on the table between them. An empty pill packet.

Surtsey picked it up. Morphine. Prescription strength with Louise's name on it. The date was old, from before she went into the hospice. They monitored pain relief carefully there in case of overdoses.

'Where did you get this?' Surtsey said.

'I was tidying up this morning after they removed her. I picked her slippers up from the floor and this was inside.'

Surtsey turned the packet over. Thirty-six tablets, more than enough. Empty, out of date, her mum's name. Had she planned this all along?

'Did you tell the hospice?' Surtsey said.

'I thought I'd leave that decision to you.'

'They'll find out anyway with the post-mortem.'

Donna shook her head. 'They don't do a post-mortem unless it's suspicious.'

Surtsey remembered the nurse on the phone saying the same.

'And there isn't anything suspicious if I don't tell them?' she said.

'Exactly,' Donna said. 'Some people don't want this kind of thing out in the open. There's still a stigma. And if anyone helped they could be charged with complicity to murder.'

'Christ.'

'I know, it's crazy, but that's the law. You think they would let people end their time peacefully.'

Surtsey held the empty box like a holy relic.

'You think that's what she did?'

Donna shrugged. 'Not necessarily. She could've been taking them in dribs and drabs in addition to her hospice medication.'

They stood in silence. Surtsey looked out the window at the boatshed.

'Thank you for bringing this,' she said. 'I mean it.'

'No problem.' Donna finished her tea and rinsed the mug at the sink. 'I'd better go.'

She made towards the kitchen doorway then turned. Surtsey had followed her, and Donna placed a hand on her arm. 'If you need anything at all, just ask. I mean it.'

Surtsey saw her to the door and watched as Donna walked down the path then along the prom. She closed the door then went back to the kitchen. Picked up the tablet packet again, turned it over in her hand. She looked at the prescription label stuck on the box. One corner of it was curled away from the cardboard. All the information on the label seemed correct, but something nagged at her mind. The red of the box, that dog-eared corner of sticker.

She put the box down and finished her tea, went to the sink and rinsed the mug. She got a tea towel and dried the mug, along with Donna's and put them back in the cupboard, as if Donna had never been here. Surtsey had never been tidy before, never cleared up after herself, had allowed Louise to do all the grunt work of keeping the house ticking over. But after Louise went into St Columba's, Surtsey had taken over that role. Someone had to, or the place would go to the dogs.

She looked out the window and it came to her. She went to the table and picked up the pill box again. She'd seen it before, she recognised it. She thought hard, closed her eyes.

She ran upstairs clutching the box and burst into the bathroom. Opened the mirrored cabinet full of bottles and packets, cotton pads and nail clippers. She pulled things aside, stuff clattering into the sink, and exposed a space.

This morphine had been in their house recently. Surtsey saw it a couple of weeks ago when she opened the cabinet to get out cotton buds. That meant her mum hadn't taken it with her to the hospice when she moved in, and she hadn't been home since.

Someone else got them and gave them to her. Within the last fortnight.

She ran out the bathroom and threw open the door to Iona's room. Her sister was still crashed out on top of her covers.

'Did you do this?' Surtsey shouted, waving the empty morphine packet, now crumpled in her fist.

Iona squinted and rolled over. 'Fuck off.'

'Don't turn away from me,' Surtsey said, grabbing at her arm.

Iona curled into herself.

Surtsey threw a punch at her shoulder, connecting with the meat of it. That got her attention. Iona pulled her arm away and scuttled backwards, sitting against the headrest of her bed.

'What the hell are you talking about?'

'Mum took these,' Surtsey said, throwing the box at her.

Iona flinched and screwed her eyes shut, then opened them. 'Hang on, I'm still asleep here.'

She fumbled for the packet, looked at it but clearly couldn't focus.

'It's Mum's morphine.' Iona looked up. 'So she killed herself?'

'And you helped her do it.'

Iona shook her head.

'Don't lie to me.' Surtsey hammered her fist at Iona's chest.

Iona's hands came up to defend herself, scrambling Surtsey away. 'Get off me, psycho.'

'All that shit on the beach earlier, seeing her in the hospice, all along you were responsible for her death.'

'Whoa, I'm not responsible for anything.'

'You killed her.'

'Sur, let me speak.'

Surtsey stood over her sister, hands on hips, breathing hard. 'I don't want to hear anything you've got to say.'

'Just listen,' Iona said. She'd sharpened up, eyes wide, and she held the packet by her fingertips like it was radioactive. 'Where did you get this?'

'They found it in her room after she died.'

'And she definitely took them?'

Surtsey thought about that. 'They think so.'

Iona shook her head. 'I didn't give these to Mum.' She examined the box, ran a finger over the label. 'They're her prescription, Sur.'

'But look at the date,' Surtsey said. 'They're from before she moved up the road.'

'So?' Iona said. 'She kept hold of them, probably for this purpose.'

It was Surtsey's turn to shake her head. 'No, these were in the bathroom cabinet recently.'

'Come on, you don't know that. There's tons of junk in there.'

'I saw them,' Surtsey said. 'With that same label on them.'

'She had hundreds of pill packets,' Iona said. 'Remember? When she was managing it at home. We were swimming in pain relief and sleeping pills.'

'No,' Surtsey said. 'I know what I saw. These were in the cabinet recently. You took them and gave them to her.'

'You've lost your mind.'

Surtsey tried to keep her voice level. 'She said you went to see her two days ago. Did you?'

'Yeah.'

'Why?'

'She's my fucking mum.'

'That didn't mean anything before. You never went to see her before. Why now?'

Iona shrugged. 'I just felt like it, OK?'

Surtsey breathed through her nose. 'No. She asked you to bring these to her, and you were only too willing to help.'

'Fuck you.'

'Did you know?'

Iona stood up, faced up to her sister. 'About what?'

'About Tom being your dad?'

Iona looked incredulous. 'How could I know, you just saw me read the letter.'

'You didn't seem that surprised.'

Iona tried to touch Surtsey's arm, but she threw it off. 'I think you'd better go before you say something you regret.'

Surtsey stood her ground. 'Maybe you knew. Maybe she already told you.'

Iona shook her head. 'If I had known you were fucking my dad, don't you think I would've told you to stop?'

'Maybe there was another way,' Surtsey said. 'Maybe you killed him.'

Iona shoved her sister and Surtsey shoved back.

'Get the fuck out of my room, and get the fuck out of my life,' Iona said.

Surtsey's eyes were wide. 'It makes a lot of sense. You resented him for never being there for you. You discover that he's been spending time with me. That he loved me, not you.'

Iona threw out a hand and punched Surtsey, a swing that connected with her jaw and made spit fly from her mouth. Surtsey held her face for a moment, shaking her head.

Iona stood over her, fists clenched. 'Get out.'

Surtsey stood tall. 'No. You need to tell me the truth.'

Iona stepped back. 'I don't have to listen to this shit.'

She went to walk past her sister but Surtsey grabbed her arm and held on. Iona threw another punch to her shoulder and her grip loosened.

'Get your hands off me.'

She pulled away and ran down the stairs then straight out the door, leaving Surtsey standing there, jaw aching, tears in her eyes.

33

Doorbell. Fucking doorbell. Just one damn thing after another.

Surtsey ignored it. She was stoned, several hits to the good. Her bedroom smelt pungent. She stared at the morphine box in her hand, one of the last things her mum touched before she died. Surtsey imagined her mum's spirit imbued in the cardboard box. No schmaltzy rainbows or bubbles that people claim to see, a sign their loved ones are happy in the afterlife. Louise was alive and thriving in an empty box of painkillers.

The doorbell didn't stop.

Surtsey sat up on her bed and took a drink of water. Breathed in through her mouth, out through her nose.

Doorbell.

She put the pill box in her pocket and trudged down the stairs. Looked through the spyhole in the front door. Cops.

'Please answer the door, Miss Mackenzie.' It was the older one. Yates. What was the other one called? Something Irish and stupid.

She sniffed the air. Her nostrils were full of the stench of hash.

Fuck it.

'Hello, officers,' she said, opening the door. Her tone was perky, mocking both herself and their presence on her doorstep. 'Good news, I hope?'

'We need to speak to you again,' Yates said.

'I could use some good news,' Surtsey said, slipping past what he'd said.

'Can we come in?'

'Do you want to know why I could do with good news?'

Yates frowned. 'We either talk here or down at the station.'

'Because my mum just died,' Surtsey said, like it was the cops' fault.

Yates's eyebrows went up and down like they were trying to send a message. The other guy – Flannery on his jacket, that was it – shuffled awkwardly, looked at his scuffed Clarks shoes, fat blobs on the ends of his legs.

'I'm sorry to hear that,' Yates said like he couldn't give a shit. 'But we still need to talk to you.'

Surtsey's eyes went wide with sarcasm.

'Sure, come in, make yourself at home. Wipe your fucking feet.'

She was in no fit state for this but a large part of her didn't give a flying shit.

She walked to the living room. 'Should I rustle you both up a sandwich?'

For a moment it looked like Flannery took her offer seriously.

She glared at him and he looked away.

'Sit.'

She pointed at the sofa and threw herself into a chair. She laid the flat of her hand against her cheek, liked the coolness of her own touch. That inherited poor circulation, cold hands, warm heart, all that bullshit. Iona was straight up hot-blooded in comparison, the angry cuckoo in the nest.

'Mrs Lawrie came to see us,' Yates said.

'Good for her,' Surtsey said. The image of Alice standing with the girls on the doorstep in the night came to her and she felt a pang of something. Those girls.

'She made some accusations.'

'I'm sure she did.'

'She thinks you killed her husband.'

'That's what she told me.'

'When?'

'Last night. She came to the house with the girls. She was drunk.' Surtsey thought about mentioning that she had driven, but didn't.

'Why didn't you report that to us?'

'Why should I?'

'It's harassment.' This was Flannery speaking for the first time.

'So the police now want to arrest everyone who has ever shouted at anyone else after a few drinks. I'm sure you have the manpower for that.'

'It's pertinent to the case,' Yates said.

'Pertinent?' Surtsey laughed. 'My God, listen to yourself.'

Yates made some notes in his wee book.

'Joined up writing, well done,' Surtsey said, craning her neck and pretending to peek.

Silence.

'Perhaps we could go over your movements on the night before Mr Lawrie's body was found,' Yates said eventually.

'We've done that,' Surtsey said, eyes narrow.

'I know, but it helps me get things straight.'

Surtsey sighed. 'I was in the office at KB.' She swallowed, her mouth dry. 'Then I was back here with Halima.'

'All night?'

'Yes.'

Yates looked at Flannery, then out the window.

'You know there's CCTV all the way along the prom,' he said.

Surtsey needed a drink of water. She chewed on her cheek.

'OK.'

'We've looked at it, of course.'

'Of course.'

'And we saw this.'

He pulled a folded sheet of A4 from his notebook, unfolded it and passed it over.

It was Surtsey pulling the boat off the sand, towards the street at the back of the house. It wasn't the clearest picture in the world but it was definitely her. The boat was identifiable too.

Surtsey sat with the piece of paper trembling in her hand.

'That is you, isn't it?' Yates said.

She tried to balance things in her mind, but it had stalled. She just stared at herself in the picture, her fingers tight on the paper. She imagined having the power to teleport away from here, or travel back in time.

'Miss Mackenzie?'

'It's me.'

She handed the paper back to Yates, who folded it away.

'I got confused,' Surtsey said. 'Got my nights mixed up. I thought that was the night before.'

'So you admit you were out on your boat the night Mr Lawrie was murdered.'

'How do you know he died that night?'

'Guys at the morgue gave us time of death. It was definitely that night.'

'And you know he was murdered?'

Yates smiled. 'Post-mortem confirmed it was assault with a blunt object, not an accident.'

'How can they know?'

Yates gave her a look. 'That's their job.'

He leaned back into the sofa like he was reeling in a fish. 'So you were out in the boat on the night in question.'

'I suppose I must've been.'

'When?'

'Between being in the office and coming home.'

'So before you were back here with your housemate.'

'Yes.'

'It's funny Miss Malik never mentioned that in her statement.'

Surtsey frowned. 'She didn't know. I was out before she got back from the office. What she said was true.'

Yates smiled. 'Very noble of you.'

'I just forgot.'

'That doesn't seem very likely.'

Surtsey wondered if the other guy was ever going to speak again.

'It's the truth,' she said.

'Were you on the Inch on the night Mr Lawrie died?'

Surtsey frowned. 'No, of course not.'

'I just presumed...'

'I went out in the boat. I got mixed up with the nights. But I wasn't anywhere near the Inch. I went east towards Fisherrow, round the coast to Cockenzie and the Pans.'

'Why?'

'Why not?' Surtsey was angry now. 'I like it out there, it clears my head. I'd just seen my dying mum and I wanted some fresh air.'

Yates shook his head, glanced at Flannery. 'You don't expect us to believe that.'

'Believe what you like.'

Surtsey had a sudden flash of Tom's collapsed skull, the blood glistening like ink on the sand, the sun low in the sky shading everything, the sea in her nostrils, the sound of gulls, the smell of them.

Tom's mobile phone, upstairs right now in her room. A simple search would find it.

'We need to bring forensics round to look at the boat,' Yates said. 'Where is it?'

Surtsey felt suddenly defeated. 'In the shed out the back.'

'And we'll need the clothes you were wearing that night.'

Surtsey couldn't summon up the energy to speak.

'Flannery will stay here to keep an eye on the boat,' Yates said. 'And you.'

'He can't stay unless I give permission,' Surtsey said. Even as she said it, it felt pointless.

'Yes he can,' Yates said. 'Unless you want to come down to the station with us now?'

Surtsey stared at him. He probably loved dominating young women in this kind of situation, using his privilege.

'You can't arrest me unless you have proof,' she said.

'Don't worry.' Yates levered himself off the sofa. 'We'll get proof.'

34

Surtsey stood in the kitchen watching the activity out the window. Three forensics in white overalls were examining the boat in the shed. They had the small door on this side open, and the large corrugated door on the other side open too, plus three spotlights on stands. It was so bright it hurt her head to look. Boxes of instruments and containers were spread on a tarpaulin in the garden. A uniformed officer stood next to them checking his phone. Surtsey tried to think if there was anything they could find out from the boat, but her mind wouldn't function.

She called Halima, trying to remember the last time she'd seen her. She still hadn't told her about Louise. Surtsey was losing control, the threads of her life unravelling.

It went to voicemail.

'Hey, Hal, it's me. Listen, I've spoken to the police again. Nothing has changed, but ... I was out in the boat that night, not on a date. You're OK, what you told them is still fine. It's just ... Mum died last night. Call me.'

She watched as one of the forensics climbed into the boat, the other two examining the hull.

Flannery had left with her clothes from that night. It was a humiliating few minutes while Surtsey raked through her wash basket, riffling through tops and dresses, bras and pants while he looked on. So much unwanted male attention, so many tiny abuses of power.

She walked upstairs to her bedroom, past Iona's door. She wondered where her sister was right now.

In her room she spotted Halima's empty hash pipe. Christ, that must've been sitting out when Flannery was in here. Lucky he spent his time ogling her and her clothes instead of paying attention. She looked round for a bag of grass but couldn't see any. Hal would have some hidden away in her room, but she didn't go and look.

The ping made her stomach sink. Tom's phone.

She lunged for it under the pillow, checked the screen:

I see the police are back.

Surtsey went to the window. A middle-aged jogger with a pot belly, an elderly woman walking two border collies. How would you recognise the person doing this anyway?

Ping:

Not long now.

Surtsey frowned, replied:

Why are you doing this?

She waited a few seconds, staring at the screen:

You'll find out soon.

Her thumbs were straight there:

What do you want?

The reply came straight away:

It's all for the best, you'll see.

Surtsey was angry now:

Best for who?

A few seconds:

You.

Surtsey couldn't think of a reply. She lifted her face from the screen and looked out of the window. The phone was sweaty in her grip. She imagined it was possessed by an evil spirit, a malevolent being trapped inside, preying on her worst fears. Maybe it was the darkness in her own mind, her Mr Hyde bubbling to the surface, or some form of wraith exacting revenge for an unknown slight.

She ran downstairs and threw open the front door, strode down the path and through the gate onto the prom. She jumped up on the sea wall. The tide was in, just twenty feet of sand then soft waves bubbling up the slope, the shush of it constant, the most familiar memory of her childhood, the backdrop to everything she'd ever done in her life.

She stared up and down the prom. No one in sight now except the dogwalker from earlier sitting on a bench outside the Dalriada. Out at sea the oil tankers were nailed to the horizon. Berwick Law like a cancerous growth to the east, the Inch over to the west mocking her.

'I'm coming for you,' Surtsey shouted at the sea.

She whipped round, faced the house then looked along the prom. 'You hear me? This is bullshit.' Her voice dropped. 'I'm coming for you.'

But she didn't even convince herself.

A phone rang in her pocket. Not Tom's, her own.

Brendan.

She puffed her cheeks out as she stared at the screen. Exhaled loudly. Thought about diverting the call but didn't.

'Hello?' she said.

Silence for a moment. She pictured him the last time they met.

'Hi, Sur.'

The sound of his voice was comforting. She'd forgotten how much she liked those Irish vowels, even just two syllables in her ear. She thought about his body next to hers.

'Brendan.'

The breeze off the sea made it hard to hear him on the other end. Salt in her nostrils, a tanginess like coke at the back of her throat as she spoke.

'How are you?' she said.

'OK. I think we should talk.'

Surtsey was still standing on the wall. She spun to look out to sea. Imagined being on the prow of an old pirate ship, an elaborate carved figurehead, pointing her chin towards the horizon. She vaguely remembered an old movie where a ship's figurehead came to life, but she couldn't remember if the animated siren was good or evil.

'I'm so sorry about everything,' she said.

'Me too.'

'Where are you?'

'In the office.'

'Is Hal there?'

A slight pause. 'No, I haven't seen her. Can you come meet me?'

Surtsey looked at the Inch, always in her eyeline as long as she stayed here. A trip across town would do her good.

'Maybe we could go for a walk,' Brendan said. 'Up Blackford Hill.'

It wasn't a random choice, it was where they'd had their first kiss, ten minutes up the road from King's Buildings. They'd wandered off together after someone's birthday drinks in the union, enjoying that first buzz, flirting madly, bumping each other deliberately, arm in arm, round the side of the observatory to the trig point where she grabbed him and made the first move.

'That would be nice,' she said.

For a moment she forgot everything else, her mum and the pills, Tom and Iona, the CCTV, police and forensics, the phone messages. She thought about Brendan and how nice it would be to walk up the hill with him again, to put her arm through his.

35

She got off the bus at the corner of Mayfield Road then crossed over to the campus. She went in past the sign and the benches. She was old enough to remember when this was just overgrown hedge and staff parking. At some point someone had decided to actually make the sciences seem appealing to prospective students.

She walked past the biology building and into the Grant Institute, glancing at the masonry above the door like she always did. Some muscle-bound Greek guy in a wreath with 'Geology 1934' carved above. She wondered who he was, maybe Atlas.

How many students and academics had walked through these doors in the last nine decades? How many had gone on to become famous in their field, or dropped out completely, turned to something else in life? Hundreds of thousands of different paths, lives that weren't hers, less complicated, less full of death.

She went up the stairs and along the corridor. The place was quiet but then it varied so much, postgrad hours weren't reliable. You did the work when you could, when the notion took you, whenever you were awake and sober, if the weather was crap. Maybe that's why it was less busy, students tended to take rare sunny days off, try to get as much vitamin D as possible before the darkness of winter.

She entered the office. She'd expected at least a couple of folk, but it was empty.

No Brendan, no Halima, no Rachel, no one else.

Maybe the Tom thing had hit everyone hard.

She walked over to Brendan's desk. His jacket was on the back of the chair, screensaver on his computer. She moved the mouse and the swirls blinked away, replaced by his desktop. Nothing out of the ordinary. Folders, files, a couple of applications open, a browser. She clicked on that. An article from *Earth* magazine on the changes in groundwater chemistry in Iceland that preceded the recent activity of Katla.

She looked at his desk. Piles of printouts, a notebook, stationery. A picture of the two of them on Blackford Hill, smiling. Not that first time, they were too drunk and too early into the relationship to take pictures. But a later visit, a trek along the Hermitage, up over the hill and down to Blackford Pond then back along the road to the office. Easy to do on a lunch break. In the picture the sun was beaming on their faces and the criss-cross sprawl of suburban houses all the way to Arthur's Seat and the castle in the distance. Trees everywhere, not just in the Meadows and Bruntsfield, but large oaks in the gardens nearby. Such a green city, so much space compared to other places. Lucky to live here.

She examined Brendan's face in the picture. Long eyelashes, those green eyes, smooth skin. So young and pretty, so much kindness. Why had she looked elsewhere for love? Why had she fallen for the oldest bullshit in the world, the attention of an older man in a position of authority? She'd felt in control of both relationships at the time, but that was a lie she told herself. It turns out she wasn't in control of anything. Just look at how quickly things fall apart.

She looked into her own eyes in the photo. Tried to see a hint of the chaos on the horizon, some foreshadowing of what was to come. But there was nothing, just happiness in the moment.

She put the picture back and wandered over to Halima's desk. No sign of activity there, no jacket, no coffee mug, her computer off.

Surtsey pulled out her phone and checked. Nothing from anyone.

She dialled Brendan's number. Maybe he'd nipped over to the union for something to eat. It took ages to connect, her signal struggling to escape the thick walls. The electronic puttering noise, interference as the call bounced around the planet.

She heard the ringtone in her ear, then a moment later the ring of Brendan's phone. Her head jerked up and she looked around the office. No one. She angled her head to hear better. On the second ring she realised it was coming from the end of the office. She began walking.

By the third ring she was back at Brendan's desk, looking around. But it wasn't there, the sound was further on. She walked. Fourth ring. Tom's office was up ahead, the door ajar. She kept walking. By the fifth ring she'd run out of open-plan space. The ring was louder but she wasn't at it yet. She could see into Tom's office through the window, but didn't see anyone.

'Brendan?'

Another ring. She still had the phone to her ear for some reason, the tone like a ghost, echoed in the real world by the phone at the other end. She imagined a thin thread connecting the two, rocketing into the atmosphere then back down, tunnelling through the roof of the building to get back in.

She put a hand on the door. Another ring.

'Brendan.'

She blinked then pushed.

Eighth ring, clear now.

Coming from Brendan's body lying on the floor. His head was caved in on the left hand side, the scalp coming away from the bone underneath, blood streaked down his face and thicker in a pool under his neck.

Surtsey lowered the phone from her ear but she could still hear both rings, the signal and the reply. She took a step forward. Brendan's eyes were open. His face wasn't filled with shock or contorted in pain, just blank, like he was daydreaming.

Surtsey could see brain. Shit, that was his brain where his skull should've been. Blood had already coagulated around his hair on the side of his head. His ear was untouched and Surtsey focussed on that. How could someone's head be destroyed, but their ear still intact? How was any of this real?

The phone finally stopped ringing in Brendan's pocket. Surtsey looked at her own phone. She could hear that it had gone to voicemail. Brendan's voice. Leave a message after the tone. She ended the call.

Blood rushed to her face. Her eyelids felt heavy and she lost focus for a second.

She looked around the office. Everything seemed normal. Then she spotted it. The large piece of white volcanic quartz Tom had used as a paperweight was sitting out of place, in the middle of the desk.

And its nearest edge was dark red.

Surtsey stared at it for a long time in silence.

Then she looked at Brendan.

Then she dialled.

36

Yates' lips were moving but she couldn't make out what he was saying. Just muffled vowels like the sound was turned down on the world. She looked around. The station interview room was a low-quality office space, stained ceiling tiles, laminate floor, plastic and metal furniture. A long strip light made everything too sharp. It felt like a job interview. She could see the police station car park out of the window, where a male and female officer were leaning against a squad car, their body language flirty. Beyond that was Beach Lane Social Club, sclaffy and beaten up, then the small, litter-strewn alleyway that led to Towerbank Primary and the beach. This was the scruffier end of the prom, away from the gentrified terraces of Joppa, the amusements at the bottom of the road attracting wayward teenagers.

She thought about Brendan's stare. She closed her eyes but that made it worse, made the image pull into focus. So she opened them again and looked at Yates and Flannery across the desk.

Flannery was faffing with the recording machine on the desk. Amazing they still used cassettes in this day and age. Such a weird concept, recording sounds onto magnetic tape.

Through the fog she realised someone was saying her name. She touched her hair, flicked it behind her ear, just to make sure her hands were real, that she could feel something. She imagined Brendan touching her in bed, a stroke of the upper arm, his fingers walking down to her thigh. Like he was tracing a path across an unpopulated place.

She saw the mess of hair and skin. Blood, bone and brains. The bloodied piece of quartz on the desk. His phone ringing in his pocket, never answered. His voicemail message all that was left of him. She suddenly had the urge to call him now, hear that voice again. How long would it be available? Could she call him and hear his voice for the next few weeks, months, years? Keep him alive forever?

Then she thought of Tom, and her mum. Their phones and voice-mails. She could keep all of them alive with a few simple calls – leave long messages about her day, ask how they were doing, make plans to meet up over coffee or wine.

The long, loud beep from the cassette machine broke through the fog.

Yates said some official stuff as a red light flashed on the tape player.

He placed his hands on the table. 'Tell us how you came to find Brendan's body.'

This was easy, just tell them everything, the truth. This time.

'I said already,' Surtsey said.

'Tell us again.'

Same tactic as before, trying to trip her up. But there was nothing to trip up. She gritted her teeth. She would be let go. This was all a mistake, the whole thing from day one. Why couldn't Tom have just been alive when she got to the Inch? Then maybe her mum would still be here, and Brendan, and Halima and Iona. Where the hell was Halima? Surely she should've been in the office, she should've been the one to find Brendan, she should've been sitting here getting bullshit from two police officers who didn't have a clue about anything.

'He called me,' Surtsey said. 'Wanted to meet up.'

'At the Grant Institute in King's Buildings?'

'At the office, yes.'

'Did that seem normal?'

Surtsey touched her eyebrow with her fingertips. Shivered at the feel of it. 'He wanted to talk about us.'

'Your relationship?' Yates was doing all the talking. Flannery just sat there like a sack of tatties, staring at her.

'Yes.'

'How was your relationship with Mr Curtis?'

'We split up.'

'When?'

'When he found out about Tom.'

'Mr Lawrie?'

'Of course,' Surtsey said. 'You think I was fucking a bunch of Toms?'

Yates narrowed his eyes. 'I don't know about your relationships with men.'

'Fuck you,' Surtsey said. 'You think I'm a slut, is that what you're saying?'

Yates glanced at the cassette recorder. Waited.

'So, you and Brendan split up,' he said.

Surtsey pulled her earlobe. 'Yes.'

'Who ended it?'

'He did.'

'When he found out you'd been having relations with Mr Lawrie.'

'"Having relations"?' Surtsey said.

'Well, how would you describe your relationship, Miss Mackenzie?'

'It's "Ms Mackenzie", thank you. We were sleeping together.'

Yates consulted the notepad in front of him, ran a pencil in a line. Surtsey couldn't see if he was scoring something out or underlining it.

'Do you think Brendan wanted to patch things up with you?'

Surtsey sat for a moment looking at Yates, then the tape machine. 'I don't know. Maybe.'

'And did you want to patch things up?'

'Yes,' she said. 'I think so.'

'You don't seem very sure.'

'I miss him.' She pictured his body on the floor in Tom's office. That stare.

'What makes you think he wanted to get back together with you?' Yates said.

'He mentioned going for a walk up Blackford Hill to the observatory. That's where we went on our first date. I thought maybe he wanted to remind us of that.'

Yates made another pencil mark on the pad. Flannery never took his eyes off Surtsey.

'What next?' Yates said.

Surtsey shook her head. 'I got the bus over, went to the office, couldn't find him. So I phoned and heard his mobile ringing. I went to Tom's office and...'

The slightest movement of Yates's head. 'You didn't touch him?'

'No.'

'Not at all?'

'I said no.'

'Did you touch anything else in Mr Lawrie's office?'

'No.'

'Are you sure?'

'Christ, I'm sure, OK?' She could feel her eyes wet, tried to contain the tears. No use showing these two any weakness. 'It was the paperweight, right?'

Flannery seemed to wake up. 'Sorry?'

'He was hit on the head with the paperweight,' Surtsey said. 'Wasn't he?'

A glance between the two of them. 'What makes you say that?'

'It was bloody. Heavy and sharp. I saw the state of Brendan's head. It doesn't take a genius to work it out.'

Yates sighed. 'We leave the forensic stuff to the experts, Ms Mackenzie.' He made a show of that 'Ms', zedding it out long and sarcastic. He peered at her. 'You don't seem very upset.'

'Should I be gnashing my teeth and tearing my hair out? Is that what good girlfriends do?'

Yates raised his eyebrows, a smile to Flannery. 'I just thought you might be more upset by your boyfriend's death, that's all.'

Surtsey tightened her mouth. 'You don't know me. You don't get to have an opinion about how I react to things.'

She sat back in the seat, felt the metal frame against her spine. 'Can I go?'

Yates laughed. He lifted his hands from the table.

'People keep dying around you, Surtsey,' he said. She noted the use of her first name, tried to think if that was significant. 'That's a problem in my line of work.'

'I wasn't near either of them when they died,' Surtsey said.

'That remains to be seen.'

'I'm telling you I wasn't.'

'But we can't just take your word for it.'

'Do you have any evidence?'

A look from Flannery to Yates suggested they hadn't had much luck.

'We know you were on your boat in the Forth on the night Tom died,' Yates said.

'So, no evidence.'

'And you discovered Brendan's body.'

'Again, no evidence of me doing anything wrong.'

'Then there's your mother.'

Surtsey felt a tremor in her legs and wondered if it was a small quake. She stared at the men, flushed cheeks and shaving rashes on their necks, white shirts too tight across bellies.

'Don't bring Mum into this.' She spoke as calmly as she could manage.

'That's three people close to you who have died in the last four days.'

'I'm warning you.'

Flannery guffawed at that. Surtsey was shocked at the sound.

'You're warning us?' he said, suddenly animated. 'We're the police, darling.'

Yates frowned at him, then at the tape machine.

'Don't fucking darling me,' Surtsey said.

'Language,' Flannery said, drenched in sarcasm.

'Fuck you.'

Flannery sank back in his seat smiling as Yates lifted a hand to quieten them both.

Surtsey turned to him. 'And fuck you, too. Are you suggesting I had something to do with my own mum's death? You sick bastard.'

'Miss Mackenzie, please,' Yates said.

Surtsey's hand was at her neck as if she was being choked. She pushed her chair back with a scrape on the thin carpet and lowered her head to her knees, heaved air into her lungs. She blinked three times and black spots drifted across her eyeline. She could see the cops' shoes under the desk, worn brown leather, square toes. She concentrated on the frayed lace of Flannery's left shoe but it went out of focus. She realised she hadn't breathed in a while and sucked in air. Eventually the dots disappeared from her vision and her head stopped throbbing. She sat up and leaned back in her seat. The two cops looked at her like her hair was made of snakes.

'We spoke to your housemate, Miss Malik.'

Surtsey's eyes widened. 'Where is she?'

'At home.'

'But I was just there.'

'It seems you missed her.'

'Is she OK?'

'Why wouldn't she be OK?' Yates said, eyes like slits.

'I just haven't seen her. Maybe she's avoiding me.'

'Why would she avoid you?'

Surtsey stared at Yates. 'No idea.'

Yates consulted his notes. 'She confirmed your new, improved alibi – that you were out in the boat earlier and had forgotten. It seems she forgot as well, until recently.'

'There you go.'

'It stinks,' Yates said, sighing. 'It'll never stand up in court.'

'I'm innocent,' Surtsey said. 'And you don't have any evidence against me.'

'We're working on that,' Flannery said.

'Good for you.'

Yates took over. 'We should have the results from the boat and your clothing in the next few hours. That will be interesting.'

'You think?'

'And we have this,' he said, lifting a piece of typed paper from the desk. 'It's a warrant to search your house.'

'This is harassment.'

'You'd know it if we were harassing you,' Flannery said.

Yates frowned and shook his head at his colleague.

Surtsey felt weariness in her bones. She eased out of the seat and stood up, which took the cops by surprise.

'Are we done?'

'Sit down,' Yates said.

'Are you going to arrest me?'

Yates stared at her for a long time before shaking his head. 'Not yet.'

'Then I'm leaving.'

She walked towards the door, hands shaking, legs weak. She made it out of the room, down the corridor and round the corner before she burst into tears.

37

She stood blinking like an idiot outside the police station. She checked her watch but didn't register what it said. She turned to look at the station, at the clock tower of the old Victorian building. It looked like something from a 70s kids' show. She couldn't make out the hands of the clock from this angle, her eyes still blurry with tears. She had to shade her eyes from the fuzz of the bright sky beyond, high cloud like muslin draped over the planet.

Two old women were sitting on the bench outside the station having a fag. One had a tartan trolley for her shopping, the other a metal walking stick with a rubber stopper on the end.

'You all right, love?'

Surtsey tried to focus. 'What?'

'Saw you come out the station, just checking you're all right.'

Surtsey shook her head. 'Fine.'

'Hey.' This was from behind her, loud and in her direction.

Surtsey turned and saw Alice clambering out of her car parked at the bus stop across the road. The windows were wound down and Surtsey could see the girls in the back in their booster seats. Belle was chomping on a Freddo and Gracie was looking sternly at her mum's back.

Alice barely glanced along the road then ran across between a white van and a bus. She landed on the pavement in front of Surtsey, manic look on her face.

'What are you doing?' she said.

'What do you mean?'

'You can't leave the station.'

Surtsey felt sorry for her, everything she'd gone through, but she was angry too. Fuck this bitch haranguing her all the time, putting her own kids at risk, building up emotional scars for them in the future.

'They've arrested you, how can they let you go?'

'They haven't arrested me.'

She couldn't quite believe it herself, that they'd let her walk out of the station. But they needed more evidence. Maybe they would get it, maybe they wouldn't, maybe they would make it up. She couldn't think of any possible way this could all end. A purgatory of dead friends, lovers and family parading past her every day, casting accusing looks in her direction.

The slap came and she welcomed it, didn't flinch, kept her chin out in case Alice wanted another crack at it.

'Christ,' said the lady with the shopping bag.

Surtsey looked over the road and caught Gracie's eye. Nine years old. Tom had talked about the girls all the time, besotted with them. She hadn't minded at all. It reminded her that what the two of them had wasn't permanent, there was no way he was going to leave Alice because it would mean leaving them. That was fine. It showed he could love unconditionally, that he had a big heart. But now this whole thing with Iona, what the hell did that mean? Did he know about her? Surely not, or how could he be sleeping with Surtsey? Louise's letter hadn't said if she'd told him. If he knew, then he was the biggest arsehole alive. Well, dead. And either way, he had been cheating on his wife for two and a half decades. But for all that maybe he was a good dad. And now his girls had no dad; that was the worst thing in all this. A lost husband or lover or boyfriend, you come to terms with that eventually. A lost parent, well, Surtsey could relate to that now. And Iona. They were both the same as Alice's girls, left to fend for themselves in the world.

Gracie was stony-faced, Belle still oblivious, looking at herself in the rear-view mirror, sticking her chocolatey tongue out.

'Your daughter is watching,' Surtsey said.

'Good,' Alice said. 'I want her to see what happens to the fucking slut who killed her dad.'

'I didn't kill Tom.'

'Of course you did,' Alice said. 'Just like you killed your Irish boyfriend.'

Surtsey frowned. 'How do you know about Brendan?'

'You're evil and I'm on to you. I can't believe the police let you go.'

Surtsey stared at her. Red cheeks, gin breath, haphazard make-up. 'Maybe the police should interview you.'

'Why?'

'You seem to know a lot about me and Brendan, that's all.'

Alice twisted at her own wrist. 'I'm going to make sure they lock you up.'

'Is that what you've been doing?' Surtsey said. 'Setting me up?'

Alice stepped closer, the alcohol rank. 'If they don't deal with you, I will.'

'Like you dealt with Tom and Brendan?'

Alice shoved Surtsey hard so that she stumbled back into the women behind her.

'Hey,' Tartan Bag said.

Surtsey struggled to right herself as Alice turned and stormed across the road without even looking at traffic. In the car, Gracie had turned the other way, as if she wasn't a part of this.

38

She cut down past McColl's and the back of Scotmid, through double-parked streets. Like a bird with a homing instinct she headed for the beach, the prom and the sight of the Forth. A view that included the Inch, a place that used to feel like a haven for her.

As she was passing the boarded-up old bingo hall, the earth shook. Another tremor, Christ. How many was that since the big one a few days ago? This was stronger than the last few aftershocks, her balance shifting as she splayed her feet and held her hands out. Aftershock was the wrong word, these quakes happened any time and they didn't follow a pattern. So much effort went into understanding seismology, geophysics and the rest, and yet it was still so spurious, no way of predicting when and where an earthquake would strike. The world shrugged off all their attempts to understand it and Surtsey had respect for that. Screw us, it was saying, we were worthless specks on the surface of the planet.

She caught the eye of a young mum pushing a girl on a trike who'd stopped to hold a railing, using her other hand to keep the trike still. The tremor lasted a few more seconds, then the buzz in the air afterwards, an expectation of more mixed with the vacuum left behind. The woman shook her head and grimaced as her daughter looked puzzled about why she wasn't able to go forward. She pushed on the pedals but her mum held her back. Surtsey shook her head at the woman and turned down Bath Street, pulling her phone out and dialling.

Ring tone then Halima's voicemail.

'My God, Hal, where are you?' Surtsey said. 'Call me.'

Another tremor made her stomach drop. Her hand went out but only found a ragged hedge. Her legs shook from stress as much as the earthquake. She thought she might be sick. The world was trying to shake her off into space. The planet had finally had enough of the billions of parasites on its surface, it was ready to start again, shake itself clean.

Then the weird stability afterwards, silence after noise.

Bile rose from her stomach up her throat. She spat on the pavement and pushed her hair away from her face.

She began again down Bath Street then stopped outside the Espy. Stared at the chipped paint on the wooden doors for a moment then pushed them open. She scanned the bar. No sign of Iona, just the lanky Canadian guy she sometimes fucked, shaved hair on one side and emo tattoos sleeved up his arm.

'Is Iona here?' she said.

He looked up from his phone, glanced around. 'She didn't come in for her shift. I'm covering for her.'

Surtsey stared at the gantry of spirits behind him, tempted.

'If you see her,' Emo said, 'tell her she owes me one.'

Surtsey pulled her phone out and called. Iona's voicemail. Christ, where was everybody? 'Call me, we need to talk.'

She rubbed at her forehead and looked at her phone. Checked social media for any posts by Hal or Iona. Nothing. She checked her messages, even though she knew neither had been in touch. Flicked to the last messages from Tom and Brendan, then flicked out. What was she doing to herself?

She pushed open the door, breathed in the salty air then headed along the prom.

The New Thule protestors were outside the boat enclosure, claiming the earth was offended by humanity. Maybe they had a point, she thought, maybe they were right all along. There were twenty of them clustered in front of the Beach House café, which couldn't be good for business. They were subdued, maybe by the recent quakes, wondering what their earth mother was trying to tell them. She pushed through them looking for Bastian, wondering about him and Iona, but she couldn't see him. She took a leaflet from a young man with thick hoops stretching his earlobes open. She crumpled the leaflet and threw it in a bin. She walked on, hunched with her hands in her pockets, daring the earth to unsettle her again.

She rubbed at her cheek where Alice had slapped her. The blood was still raised at the skin and she wondered if it would leave a mark. Maybe she could have her charged with assault. But Surtsey knew she deserved it. She might not have killed Tom but she felt responsible, felt as if she'd started this whole chain of events where everyone around her was dying.

She walked past the swimming pool where her mum had taught her to swim and kept walking. The sun was high to her right, making her squint as she came out of the building's shadow. The Inch was behind her, nagging at her mind. She went past the ice cream van, thought about how many hundreds of cones she'd eaten from there. With her mum, with Iona, more recently with Hal or Brendan. Every step she took retraced a thousand previous walks, over and over, the promenade defining her childhood, her adulthood, her recent descent. The sea always changing, the sand shifting, the light dancing or brooding, the haar sometimes in, snowstorms bristling the sand, the wind throwing oil drums or dead seals or once a rotting whale carcass onto the shore. Always different, always unexpected, yet somehow reliable too, always there for her.

She passed the hospice and couldn't help looking at her mum's window. She stopped in her tracks like she'd hit a wall. An old woman was sitting in a wheelchair at the window, thin white hair in wisps from her head, like lightning tracers. She had bags under deep-set eyes and thick creases in her forehead, and she smiled at Surtsey, who just stood there. Of course they would reassign the room, they were a business. Of course some other sad, dying person would love to have Louise's sea view. But Surtsey hadn't got her head round that yet. She'd expected to see the room empty, but now some cancerous old witch was sitting at her mum's window looking at the view, sleeping in her mum's bed and using her mum's bedpan to piss in if she couldn't make it to the toilet. The old woman raised a spindly hand and waved, more of a muscle tremor than anything. Surtsey put on a smile and waved back, then wiped tears from her face and walked on. She gazed at the sea, a flat sheet of hammered silver.

She went through the contacts on her phone and called Mum.

Voicemail. Her mum's voice. 'I can't get to the phone right now, leave a message and I'll get back to you.'

Then the bit about re-recording your message, followed by the tone. Silence.

'I miss you, Mum,' Surtsey said. 'I need you. Come back to me, please.'

She was crying hard now.

'I'm such a mess, my God, you would be so disappointed.'

She laughed and sniffed, wiped away tears with the heel of her hand.

'You would tell me to get my shit together but you would give me a hug too. Christ, I need that right now.'

A crackle on the line, a ghost in the ether.

'I'm so sorry.'

She ended the call and stood there, trying to get her breathing back to normal, clutching her phone like a rare fossil.

She walked towards home. As she walked she pictured her mum in their house, shouting to her and Iona to brush their teeth and get their shoes on, they were late for school. Or telling them their tea was ready. Or patting them on the bum as they walked up the stairs in their jammies, trailing teddies. Just life, the stuff we ignore because it's so commonplace. The stuff that matters.

She reached her house and stopped. Standing on the doorstep was Donna, a smile on her face and a bottle of red wine in her hand.

39

'I'm glad you're here,' Surtsey said, as she fiddled with her key.

'Really?'

Surtsey turned and held her gaze. 'Really.'

Donna smiled. Surtsey noticed long shadows spread over the sand behind her, so it was evening. She tried to think if she'd eaten anything today.

She opened the door. 'Come in.'

Donna shuffled up the step behind her. Surtsey stopped in the doorway, grabbed her and hugged. Donna's perfume filled her nose. It was a smell she recognised but couldn't place. Maybe the same stuff Iona or Halima used. Maybe just from the hospice, smelling it in her mum's room.

She let go and smiled awkwardly.

Donna returned the smile. 'Are you OK?'

'Far from it.'

Donna waved the wine at her.

Surtsey grabbed glasses from a kitchen cupboard then headed to the living room, Donna behind. She poured glasses for them both.

Surtsey glugged away while Donna took a sip. That's right, she didn't like to get drunk, to lose control. Surtsey tried to imagine being in control and a laugh slipped from her mouth.

'What's so funny?' Donna said.

'Control.'

Donna looked confused.

Surtsey waved her glass. 'Never mind. Sit.'

They sat opposite each other, Surtsey facing the bookshelf, those family snaps scattered amongst the science books.

'Tell me about your parents,' Surtsey said.

Donna fidgeted with the stem of her glass. 'Really?'

'Unless you don't want to talk about it.'

Donna picked at the seam of her jeans. They were dirty around the bottom, her Nikes sandy too. She was wearing a nondescript T-shirt with a hoodie thrown over, dressed for comfort rather than going out. Nothing wrong with comfort. Surtsey had rarely seen her out of uniform, and she noticed that Donna looked strong, a physical presence in the living room. Beneath the flesh in that hug had been some solid muscle too. Surtsey wondered if she worked out.

'I don't really,' Donna said.

Surtsey tried to figure out why she'd invited her in. Maybe it was this: she didn't want to talk about her dead parents, and there was no great desire to share, to make their relationship about her and her troubles. She was an empty page waiting to be filled by Surtsey. A good listener, her mum would've said, perfect for nursing. A sounding board for all of Surtsey's problems. Except Surtsey couldn't tell her any of it. She briefly wondered if she should tell Donna about Tom, about finding him on the island. She said nothing.

'It's a hard time,' Donna said. 'When someone you love dies.'

'What about when several of them die?'

'What do you mean?'

Surtsey gulped wine. 'Nothing.'

'Is there something I don't know? Has something happened?'

Surtsey laughed. 'I wouldn't know where to start.'

'I'm a good listener.'

As if she'd been reading Surtsey's thoughts again. She shook her head.

Donna smiled. 'I never could've imagined at school that we would be friends.'

Surtsey supposed they were friends. What else did you call this? She needed someone to talk to and here was Donna, that's what friends did for each other. But she was using her too, an emotional sponge to soak up all the bullshit, a psychological dumping ground.

Donna looked at Surtsey's empty glass on the table and filled it.

Surtsey was in accelerated drinking mode, craving the second and third glasses, soon the tenth. She wondered if Hal had any grass in her room.

The wine was smooth going down, a decent bottle. She looked at Donna, what did she know about her? She'd barely noticed her at school, not on her radar. But that was always the way at school, you never noticed the younger ones, but younger ones always looked up to older girls. Surtsey tried to remember the incidents Donna had mentioned. Tearing strips off Donna's bully at the bonfire, standing up for her in the toilets at the school disco. The truth was that she pulled a blank, couldn't remember a thing. Partly she was drunk, but partly it was just Surtsey doing her thing, and there was ego involved in that too. She hadn't really been defending Donna by the sound of it, she had just been mouthing off on her own agenda, virtue signalling to the rest of the school.

What made a real friendship? Just time and support. And Donna had been more supportive than anyone else the last few days, helping with her mum, someone to talk to. So why not friends?

'Cheers.' Surtsey leaned forward to clink. She misread the distance and the glasses clanged together, wine sloshing on the coffee table between them.

'Cheers,' Donna said, smiling.

'Here's to being friends.' Surtsey drank.

'To friends.' Donna sipped.

Surtsey narrowed her eyes. 'You really don't like drinking, do you?'

Donna shrugged. 'Because of my mum. It killed her and I couldn't do anything to stop it. I never want to feel that powerless.'

'I get that.' Surtsey thought about Tom. Christ, the messages on his phone. All the shit with Brendan had made her forget about that.

'Just a minute,' she said, slopping her glass on the table.

She left the room and tottered upstairs.

'Are you OK?' Donna shouted up.

She checked the phone under her pillow. There was a new message:

Death follows you around, doesn't it?

She stared at it for a long time like it was a message from God. Maybe it was. How do you reply to God? And how can you make him listen?

She stood there, legs weak, craving more wine.

'Sur?'

She jumped. It was Donna in the bedroom doorway.

She held up the phone in her hand. 'God is sending me messages.'

'What?'

Surtsey laughed, aware how ridiculous it was. 'This phone is my conscience, the little devil on my shoulder.'

'You're not making any sense,' Donna said.

'Nothing makes sense.'

'Are you OK?'

Surtsey stared at the phone. She stared at it so long the screen went dark. She pressed a button to wake it up again then typed:

Fuck you.

She breathed out and looked at Donna, who was holding both wine glasses. She took hers and downed it in three gulps.

'I need some air,' she said.

40

'I really don't think this is a good idea,' Donna said.

Surtsey didn't turn around. 'Just push.'

They'd hauled the RIB across most of the beach and were almost at the water's edge. The soft dry sand was behind them, and it was easier to guide the trailer over the packed sand now underfoot. Surtsey was sweating alcohol from her pores, damp stains under her arms as she pulled the boat towards the sea.

'You've had quite a lot to drink,' Donna said.

Surtsey felt acid rise in her throat and swallowed it down.

'I'm fine,' she said over her shoulder. 'This is exactly what I need, the sea air will sort me out.'

She splashed into the edge of the water, feeling her socks squelch and the cold ripple around her shoes, penetrating the red wine glow. She kept going until the whole trailer was in the water then began untying the boat from the front end.

'Do the knots at the back,' she said.

Donna stared at her with a strange look on her face.

'There's nothing to be nervous about,' Surtsey said. She put on a pompous voice. 'I'm an experienced seafarer, don't you know.'

'It's not that,' Donna said. She still hadn't touched the ties at the back of the trailer.

'Then what?'

'All the wine.'

'So what?'

'Just, with your mum and everything.'

Surtsey stopped fiddling with the rope and looked up. 'You knew my mum as well as anyone.'

'I didn't really, she was a patient, not family.'

Surtsey waved that away. 'You saw her the other day on the Inch. She was happy, right?'

Donna nodded. 'She seemed to be.'

'She loved the water, loved the island, loved everything about being out there. I'm the same. This is what I need, Donna, trust me. I need to get out there, get away from all this.'

She waved a frantic hand at the prom, as if it was responsible for her troubles.

'Maybe another day,' Donna said. 'When you've had some sleep.'

'Fuck that,' Surtsey said. 'Sleep is the cousin of death.'

Her legs felt rooted in the sand beneath the waves lapping at her calves as if she might be stuck forever like one of those Gormley statues people kept trying to save from drowning. She imagined being made of metal, rusting over the years but unbending to the vagaries of life.

She finished undoing the knots at the front of the trailer and looked up. Donna was untying the back, good, none of this waiting till Surtsey was sober. Surtsey couldn't imagine being sober long enough to get her shit together.

The boat bobbed free of the trailer and Surtsey held the guide rope on the side.

'Get in,' she said.

'I don't know.'

Surtsey raised her eyebrows. 'I'm going out in this thing with or without you.'

Donna looked at Surtsey then out to sea in the direction of the Inch. She turned to look back at the terraces along the prom.

'OK.'

'Get in backwards, it's easier. Grip the handles at the sides then scoot over on your bum.'

They were both wet up to their knees but Surtsey could hardly feel the cold. She watched as Donna thudded into the boat. She pulled herself in, landing with a flap of limbs in Donna's lap. She looked up at her, silhouetted by the evening sky, her face in darkness.

'Excuse me.' She smiled, righting herself.

She clambered to the back and started the engine. Spray kicked up and they were off, heading into the low waves, bouncing with each encounter.

Donna looked back.

'Will the trailer be all right?'

'Tide's going out, it's fine.'

Surtsey had no idea if that was right, hadn't checked the tides.

Donna looked around. 'Lifejackets?'

Surtsey made a show of inspecting the interior of the boat. 'Don't see any.'

'Christ, Sur.'

It felt strange hearing Donna call her by her nickname, but not bad. Why not, they were friends now.

They were in open water, two hundred yards from land. Surtsey breathed salt into her nostrils, but her head stayed foggy. Her legs were heavy. She'd noticed it earlier trudging through the sand, but they felt like lead weights now. She must be drunker than she thought.

Something occurred to her.

'We didn't bring any wine.'

Donna shook her head. 'You've had enough.'

Surtsey made a panting sound, her tongue was furry and felt too big for her mouth. 'I'm thirsty.'

'You're fine.'

They rattled along, spray in their faces, the land a thinning line behind them. Surtsey turned the rudder, pointed west towards the Inch.

'What are you doing?' Donna said.

'What do you think?'

'Is that a good idea?'

'Come on, Donna, you always knew that's where we...' Her mouth stopped working for a second. Surtsey frowned and swallowed. It was hard work. She tried to get her tongue into gear. 'Where we ... were headed...'

Surtsey's hand slipped from the rudder. She tried to turn and look behind her but her head was immensely heavy, a rock that her neck couldn't support. She couldn't swallow either. She tried to grab the rudder handle again but her arm wouldn't move, the signal from her brain didn't reach her body. It was so hard to breathe, her lungs concrete, pressure on her chest. She closed her eyes and struggled to open them again. Her mind was fog. She tried to think what she'd just been saying but couldn't remember. She felt a hand on her chin, raising her head up from her chest where it had slumped. She eventually opened her eyes.

Donna smiled at her.

'You have a little sleep,' she said, easing Surtsey's body down to lie along the seat. She took the rudder and gunned the engine. 'I'll take things from here.'

41

She couldn't breathe, arms weak in the currents, head under the surface, lungs filling with water. A giant whale came and swallowed her whole, her body tumbling over the colossal tongue and down into its gut, sloshing around, the stomach acid eating at her legs. The whale's heartbeat was thunderous making her wince in pain, her bowels shake, reverberating through her body until she thought she might break apart, her limbs floating off, her torso shredded to pieces, her head lolling around in the acrid stench of the place.

The heartbeat kept thudding away as she came round, immense throbs ricocheting from the back of her neck to her temples. Each beat made her clench her stomach and forced air out of her nose at the immediacy of the pain. She screwed her eyes tight and breathed in, concentrated on her lungs, tried to get the rhythm of them going.

Bursts of light and dark danced across her eyelids but she couldn't get her eyes open. She tried to lift a hand to her head but her arms wouldn't move. She flexed an ankle, found it was constrained. She badly needed to pee.

She took a few deep breaths, listening in between for any noise. A metallic creak, part of a building relaxing or contracting. A thin whisper of wind somewhere. She listened for waves but couldn't hear any.

Her eyelids fluttered open and she blinked over and over, screwing them shut again to get the blurriness away. The thump in her head was still there, a constant beat of pain. She focussed and looked around, the movement of her neck making pain soar through her again, forcing breath from her.

She knew where she was, recognised it immediately, it was the scientific hut on the Inch. She'd been here a dozen times, warmed her beans on the stove in the corner, left rock samples in the storage drawers to her left.

She was strapped to the bed. Her wrists were tied to the frame at either side with heavily knotted ropes. She had about two inches of movement from the scratchy blanket she was lying on before the ropes dug into her skin. Her feet were tied the same, through the frame at the bottom of the bed, a little looser so that she had a few more inches to move her legs, but not enough to help any.

There was only low light from the small window behind her but it was still enough to see by. There was a large rucksack on the floor by the door, the one thing that seemed out of place. She recognised everything else, the sparse furniture, the stove, the geological map on one wall. No electricity or running water, of course, a basic bothy. The only amenity was a chemical toilet outside, a few yards down the slope away from the hut. Speaking of which, her bladder screamed at her. Her headache persisted and her arms and legs felt fizzy with numbness. She opened and closed her fists, tried to get blood flowing into her arms again, curled and uncurled her toes, tried not to think about pissing herself.

The door opened.

'You're awake,' Donna said.

She looked energised, wide-eyed, small pupils. She was carrying a black canvas holdall, which she placed on the floor. She was beaming a smile as she raised her eyebrows at Surtsey.

Surtsey nodded at her wrist ties. 'What the fuck have you done?'

Donna sat on the bench that ran along the small dining table in the middle of the room. 'I didn't know when you would wake up so I couldn't take the chance.'

'What?'

'I wasn't sure how long the diazepam would take to wear off. You're only a slip of a thing and of course you were drinking a lot; that makes it harder to judge. But you've been out for a long time.' She looked at her watch. 'Almost seven hours.'

'Christ.'

'That's OK,' Donna said, crossing her legs. She nodded at the rucksack and holdall on the floor. 'It gave me plenty of time to get back and pick up some provisions.'

'This is insane,' Surtsey said. 'Let me go.'

Donna shook her head. 'I can't.'

'Why are you doing this?'

'It's for the best,' Donna said. 'I don't expect you to understand, not straight away, but you'll come to see things my way eventually.'

'What do you plan on doing, keeping me here forever?'

Donna got up and opened the rucksack. She began lifting out food, bags of rice and pasta, tins of sauce and beans, water bottles, chocolate bars and crisps, a carton of orange juice.

'You actually made it much easier,' Donna said. 'I think subconsciously you knew all along and were trying to help me.'

'You've lost your mind.'

'When I came round to your house yesterday I was all set to take you back to my place.' Donna reached deeper into the rucksack and pulled out salt and pepper, biscuits, a loaf of bread. 'But this is better. You wanted to come to the Inch and now we're here together. This place means so much to you, doesn't it?'

'Fuck you.'

'Come on,' Donna said. 'You brought me here, when you think about it. You were drunk and you wanted to bring me, your best friend, to your favourite place. All I'm doing is making sure that happened. The state you were in, you couldn't have steered the boat any longer so I had to take over.'

'Because you drugged me,' Surtsey said. 'The wine.'

'It was just to help you relax. You've been through so much recently.'

'But you drank it too.'

Donna shook her head as she arranged food on the table. 'Small sips, spat back into the glass when you weren't looking. I don't like to lose control, remember?'

Surtsey tugged at her wrist ties. 'Let me go.'

Donna smiled and shook her head. 'If you just realised this was for your own good, I wouldn't have to tie you up.'

Surtsey stared at her. 'You're insane. This is insane.'

Donna unzipped the holdall and started taking out clothes, shirts and T-shirts, underwear, jeans. Some of it was Surtsey's.

'How did you get my stuff?'

Donna dug into her pocket and pulled something out, dangled it in the air. 'I have your keys, silly.'

Surtsey's head was pounding, the base of her neck on fire. 'You can't keep me here.'

Donna put the keys away and went back to unpacking the clothes. 'It'll be fine once you come round.'

'Come round to what? Being kidnapped and held prisoner?'

Donna went over to the stove and opened it, threw in a couple of logs from a pile. She closed the door, poured some water into a pan from a ten-gallon plastic bottle on the floor then placed it on the stovetop.

'Cup of tea will sort us out.'

Surtsey tried to kick her legs, twisting her ankles inwards and out, flexing her muscles against the ropes. The effort made blood thud in her ears, flashes of white across her vision. She slumped back on the bed and breathed.

'Someone will find me,' she said. 'When they realise I've gone missing. They're probably already trying to get in touch.'

Donna got two mugs off a shelf and placed them on the table. Pulled teabags out a box and dropped them in. She looked for a teaspoon in a drawer.

'I don't think so,' she said over the rattle of cutlery.

'Iona and Hal. If I don't show up, they'll come looking for me, they'll track me down.'

Donna stopped what she was doing and turned to stare at Surtsey. She shook her head as if she was listening to a baby talk gibberish.

'When will you realise they're not your friends. They don't have your best interests at heart.'

'And you do?' Surtsey said, lifting her tied hands as far as she could.

'They won't look for you, I made sure of that.'

'What do you mean?'

Donna glanced at the water on the stove, steam starting to rise from the pan.

'They're probably still asleep for a start, I gave them twice the dose I gave you. A bit of a risk, but one worth taking.'

'You drugged them?'

Donna smiled. 'You girls really like to drink. It's so easy, just bring a bottle of wine round, make up some excuse about looking for you, then stay and have a drink. Thank goodness for screw tops, so much easier to slip something in. The two of them were gulping the stuff down like juice. They didn't care about finding you then and they won't now.'

'You were at my house with them? Where are they?'

'It's simple to get people to do what you want. The diazepam worked very quickly. They both crashed out, I just helped them to bed.'

'Wait,' Surtsey said. 'They were in the house when we were back there?'

Donna nodded. 'That was one thing I was worried about, that you'd check their rooms. That's why I followed you upstairs.'

Surtsey swallowed hard. 'They'll come looking for me.'

'I don't think so. I texted from your phone, told them you were going away for a while to clear your head, they weren't to get in touch. They'll understand your need for space after everything you've been through.'

Surtsey felt a tremor through her body. She lay there working it out for a moment, thinking what to say. 'It was all you.'

Donna was at the stove, water burbling away. She lifted the pan to the table and poured water into the mugs. She stood holding the pan with the remains of the boiling water in it.

'What?'

'Tom. The messages on his phone. You killed him.'

Donna still had the pan in her hand, water sloshing as she gesticulated.

'He wasn't right for you, Sur, anyone could see that.'

'Oh God.'

'A married man twice your age, and your boss? What a cliché. You could do so much better.'

'Like you, you mean?'

Donna screwed her nose up and her brow creased. 'I'm not like that. It's not about that.'

'How did you know about me and Tom?'

Donna put the pan back on the stove and stirred the mugs. She lifted the teabags out and dumped them in an empty Asda bag. She got the milk from the table, popped the seal and poured.

'I've been looking after you for a long time, making sure you're OK.'

'Spying on me?'

Donna shook her head. 'It's not spying if you do it for the right reasons. It's observing.'

'But you didn't just observe,' Surtsey said, her voice shaking. 'You killed him. You smashed his head in with a rock.'

Donna brought both mugs to the edge of the table nearest the bunks and sat on the bench.

'The look on his face was pathetic,' she said. 'So eager to see his secret lover, so needy. I've no idea what you saw in him.'

Surtsey frowned. 'How did you have the number of his phone?'

Donna smiled. 'It was on the beach when you found him, wasn't it? I copied the number then put it there afterwards, so you would pick it up, I knew you wouldn't leave it lying around so that people knew about the two of you. Then I could be in touch with you.'

'You're a murderer and a psychopath.'

Donna picked up one of the mugs and threw the tea in Surtsey's face. Her lips and eyes burned as she spluttered. It wasn't quite boiling, the milk had taken the edge off, but it stung like crazy. Surtsey felt the blood rise to the skin on her neck and cheek where it had taken the brunt of it.

Donna leaned over her, pointing. 'I'm the only friend you've got, remember that. The sooner you come to terms with it the better.' She stepped away from the bed. 'Those others are all wrong. That bitch Halima, your slut of a sister. You said yourself she's useless and selfish.

Tom was ridiculous, I felt embarrassed for you. No wonder you kept it a secret. And Brendan.'

'He never did anything wrong.'

'He wasn't good enough for you.'

'According to you, no one is good enough for me.'

Donna smiled. 'Except me.'

'So you do fancy me.'

'I've told you already I'm not like that. We're friends.'

Surtsey's face was singing with pain. 'Friends don't tie each other up.'

Donna sat down and sipped her tea.

'It's only temporary, until you come to your senses.'

'What if I never do?'

'You will.' Donna looked out the window. 'Besides, you can't go back now anyway.'

'What do you mean?'

'The police will arrest you for murder.'

Surtsey stared at her. 'What have you done?'

'I had to time it all right,' Donna said. 'I've been drip-feeding them leads about you, but I couldn't have them arrest you before I got a chance to get you. Now you're safe, they'll soon get an anonymous tip off and find Tom's boat in Fisherrow and guess what? Your DNA will be all over it. And forensics at Brendan's death will find traces of you too.'

Surtsey realised she'd been straining against her ties, her head raised from the thin pillow. She flopped onto the bed and breathed out.

'I'm sorry about the tea,' Donna said. 'But you made me so cross.'

Something suddenly occurred to Surtsey. 'Oh, shit. Mum.'

Donna pursed her lips. 'No.' She looked down at her lap. 'She did that herself.'

'I don't believe you.'

'She was very brave, your mum. Much stronger than mine.'

'You gave her the pills from our bathroom,' Surtsey said. 'You took them when you were at my house.'

Donna got up. 'Are you hungry? I'm hungry. A cheese sandwich, I think.'

'Tell me, please.'

Donna opened the loaf of bread, got a knife and ripped open a pack of cheddar.

'Louise wanted to die,' she said, buttering a slice of bread. 'In her own way, at her own time. She knew you wouldn't help her, and she didn't want to ask you anyway. So I helped her. I was going to give her an overdose from the medical stores, but they would've suspected me. Louise told me about the pills in your house.'

'I don't believe you, she wouldn't have gone like that without saying goodbye.'

'What do you think our trip here was?' Donna sliced cheese and placed it on the bread. 'You saw how happy she was.'

'Why should I believe you?' Surtsey said. 'After everything you've done.'

'You can choose to believe me or not,' Donna said, adding the second bread slice and halving the sandwich. 'I know the truth. She wanted to end it herself and I helped. I did what you couldn't do because you're family. I did you a favour.'

'The post-mortem will find out the truth.'

Donna put both sandwich halves on a plate and came over to the bed. 'There's no post-mortem, you know that. A terminally ill patient dies in a hospice during the night. Hardly grounds for suspicion.'

She held out half a sandwich. 'Here, you need to eat.'

'Go to hell.'

Donna sighed and sat down, took a large bite from the sandwich and chewed. After a few moments she spoke. 'I don't expect you to come round straight away but a bit of appreciation wouldn't hurt.'

'You're insane.'

'After all I've done for you.'

Surtsey felt the pressure on her bladder, all that wine still sloshing around. She thought of the chemical toilet just outside the hut. A chance to get away.

'I need to pee.'

Donna frowned. 'It can wait until I finish this.'

'I really need to go.'

Donna brushed crumbs from her hands and stood up. She went to the holdall and pulled out something white and plastic. A bedpan.

'No,' Surtsey said. 'I need to go to the toilet.'

'Nonsense, I can't take that chance. This will be fine.'

'I can't go in that.'

'Of course you can, there's no need to be embarrassed, we're friends. I've done this a million times with patients. I'll be discreet, I promise.'

Donna came to the bed and placed the bedpan on the blanket. She reached for the button on Surtsey's jeans and undid them.

Surtsey squirmed. 'I've changed my mind, I don't need.'

'Don't be silly, it's just me.'

Donna pulled her jeans and pants down to her tied ankles.

Surtsey felt the draft on her legs, goosebumps on her skin at the exposure. 'Don't.'

Donna pushed at her buttocks, rolled her torso over as far as it would go with the constrained legs, slid the bedpan under her bum and rolled her back.

'On you go.'

'I can't.'

Donna smiled. 'I won't look, how about that.'

She turned and faced the door of the bothy.

Surtsey released her bladder, the relief overwhelming. So humiliating. She couldn't get her legs spread enough and the pee ran in rivulets down the inside of her thighs and buttocks into the bedpan, uncomfortable warmth mixed with shame and relief. She seemed to pee forever and worried the bedpan would overflow. Eventually the stream stopped, the last drips trickling into the pan wedged under her bum.

Donna turned. 'Good girl.'

She rolled Surtsey over and removed the bedpan, placing it on the floor. She went to the holdall and took out toilet roll and wet wipes.

'I'll sort you,' she said. She dabbed with folded up squares of toilet paper, then a cold wipe against Surtsey's buttocks. She dropped the paper and wipes in the bedpan and eased Surtsey's hips straight. Her fingers lingered on the skin of her waist for a moment, then she went to the bottom of the bed and wriggled Surtsey's pants and trousers up, Surtsey lifting her hips to let her.

'I'll get rid of this,' Donna said, picking up the bedpan from the floor and heading out the door, which stayed open.

Surtsey angled her head to see out. She could make out a swathe of volcanic rock, the black bubbles and jags of it sweeping towards shore. She looked for the jetty, a boat, anything out on the water, but couldn't see from here. She strained at her wrist and ankle ties but they didn't budge. She flopped back on the bed exhausted, head thumping, heart jumping in her ribs, the skin on her face tingling.

Donna filled the doorway, silhouetted against the thin cloud outside, the shimmering sea. Surtsey tried to think what time it was, what day even. She'd slept for seven hours, at least that's what Donna said. Did that mean it was early morning of the next day?

'What's your plan?' she said, as Donna came in and pulled the door behind her.

'What do you mean?'

'We can't stay here forever.'

'Why not?'

Surtsey shook her head. 'There will a research team on the island soon.' She raised her eyes to the roof, thinking. 'The next one is scheduled for tomorrow, I think. They'll come to the hut.'

Donna laughed. 'It's so sweet you think you can lie to me.'

'I'm not lying.'

'I checked the research trip schedule online, there isn't one for ten days. But it doesn't matter, the police have put a stop to any island visits because it's a crime scene.'

'But they already did forensic tests.'

Donna shrugged. 'Who knows? Anyway, we won't be discovered for a long time, and by then I'll have another plan.'

Surtsey was about to speak when the ground shook under them. Another tremor. Donna braced herself against the roof and the doorframe. Surtsey felt vulnerable, spread-eagle on the bed. The aluminium legs of the bed scraped and rattled against the concrete floor and the bed shifted a couple of inches away from the wall and into the room.

The quake kept going. Normally a few seconds and these shocks were over but this grumbled on, a low level buzz of the earth amplifying to a shiver then jerks, each one making Surtsey's muscles clench. The loaf of bread fell over on the table, the knife bumped off the plate where it had been placed, the water bottles arranged along the wall shimmied and danced, nudging each other as if sharing a secret. As long as the bothy didn't shake apart, as long as the stove stayed in one piece and the windows in their frames, they were OK.

After a minute or more a sudden jerk made the bed jump an inch, then there was stillness. Surtsey's head thumped with the blood coursing round her veins, her heart frantic, stomach tight.

Donna's eyes were wide, a grin on her face as if they'd shared a secret. 'That was something.'

Surtsey looked at her wrists. 'You have to untie me, it's not safe.'

Donna patted the concrete wall. 'You're OK, this thing will stand up to more than that.'

'What if it doesn't, what if there are more quakes? Stronger ones?'

Donna shook her head. 'I can't let you go.'

She looked around the room, assessing it, checking for anything out of order.

'Now, I have to get the rest of our provisions,' she said, reaching for the door handle. 'I won't be long. Are you sure you don't want anything to eat?'

Surtsey stared at her for a long time then shook her head.

Donna opened the door and stepped into the doorway. 'I'll be back in a jiffy.'

The door closed behind her and Surtsey heard the key turn in the lock.

42

She looked around for something to help her. Flexed her wrists in turn, hoping the ropes had loosened, but she couldn't feel any difference. She did the same with her legs, nothing. She craned her neck to survey the room. The stove was still going, the water pan on the side cooling. The rucksack and the holdall on the floor. She wondered if Donna had unpacked everything, there must be something she could use. She looked at the table again. Two mugs, the open cheese packet, the remains of a sandwich.

The knife. Just a butter knife, but a knife all the same. It had bumped off the plate in the tremor and was sitting near the edge of the table about three feet away from her. It might as well have been a million miles.

Surtsey looked at the door. She wondered what Donna meant by getting the rest of the provisions. Was she only away for a few minutes to the boat to bring more bags, or did she have to leave the island and head back to Portobello? The difference between ten minutes and two hours.

Surtsey put her head back on the pillow and thought. She summoned all her energy and threw her body up and to the left. The bed scraped an inch to the left with her. Holy shit, this could work. She tried to calm her breath, get her energy back, then made the same manoeuvre again. The bed jumped again, landing another fraction closer to the table and the knife. The table was low, only an inch or two higher than the bed frame. The knife was sitting on the edge, almost hanging over. If she managed to position the bed in the right place, she might be able to scoop it with her fingers into her grasp.

She heaved again and the bed rattled and shifted. It was noisy, the metal legs against the concrete floor, and Surtsey waited a moment afterwards, listening for anything from outside. But all she could hear were gulls and crows.

She repeated the movement again and again. She had to presume Donna would be back sooner rather than later, so she worked as fast as possible. Each exertion was taking its toll, decreasing her energy levels, the ropes digging into her wrists and ankles with every tiny jump. She found it easier to swing the bottom half of the bed with one heave then the top half of the bed in the next, easing the strain on her a little and effectively walking the bed over to the table.

Heave after heave, Surtsey arched then thrashed her back against the covers, the bed creeping towards the table with each effort until finally she was almost there. She stretched her left hand out as far as it could go, brushed at the end of the knife handle with her fingertips, but couldn't get any purchase.

Two more bumps, her arms and legs drained, the skin on her wrists cut by the ropes, the abrasions showing small bubbles of blood along them.

She stretched again, touched the knife, but it slipped under her finger and spun away from her. She heaved again, lower half of the bed then the upper half, another two inches closer, then she spread her fingers as wide and long as she could. Her middle finger touched the handle, pushed it down against the wooden slat of the table. She managed to get her index finger to hold the handle there as she did a desperate flick back with her middle finger, and the knife budged a couple of inches towards her. It was enough to get a grasp with both fingers. She lifted it and precariously bent her fingers until she could use her thumb to balance her grip from the other side.

She had it. She fucking had it.

She looked at the door. Maybe she had hours. Maybe she had two minutes. Maybe she had no time at all.

She flicked the knife upside down in her hand and felt under the mattress. The frame seemed solid underneath and she carefully placed the knife under the mattress then lowered the mattress back down.

She thrashed again, this time in the other direction, trying to get the bed back in place. Again, it was easier doing the top half then the bottom. She had cramp in her shoulder blades and calves, her biceps and forearms burning with the exertion every time she moved. She launched herself away from the bed again, the legs scraping against the floor but moving, an inch at a time. Despite the pain surging through her she felt energised. This was a way out, this was a possibility of escape. She had to take it.

She stopped for a second and listened. No noise outside. The air felt electric with silence after the constant grate of the bed legs on the floor. She heaved again and again, top then bottom. She was getting closer to her original position with every thrust but the bed was slightly skewed, the feet end sticking out more than the top. She didn't know exactly where she'd been before, but the angle made it obvious that the bed had moved.

She heaved her legs again, the ropes slicing into her ankles, and she grunted in pain. The bed moved, then moved again with the next effort. The bed had been up against the wall when she woke up, but the earthquake had shifted it a little. She tried to guess where it had been. Then she thought about the scraping. She looked but couldn't see any marks on the concrete.

She heaved one more time, the bed snapping to the right, further away from the table. It still hadn't quite straightened up. She was about to thrust herself upwards again when the door swung open and Donna came in carrying another holdall and a small backpack.

43

She tried to calm her breathing. Her wrists raged in pain, her ankles too, all her muscles screamed at her, but she tried to just lie there as if she'd been doing nothing. Her armpits were damp from the effort, sweat at the base of her back and between her thighs, but she hoped her face wasn't too flushed.

Donna smiled at her and put the bags down.

She looked around the room then back at Surtsey. Her eyes went to the foot of the bed, at a slight angle to the wall. She frowned. Looked at the floor. Surtsey kept her eyes on her, watching, didn't try to crane her neck or look at what Donna was seeing. Marks on the floor, something amiss in the room, the knife gone from the table.

Donna came over and stood at the foot of the bed.

She leaned down and lifted the frame, carried it to her left until it was flush with the wall.

'Stupid tremor,' she said. 'Can't have your bed bumping all the way outside now, can we?'

Her hand brushed at Surtsey's ankle. She stopped to look at the angry rope marks on the skin.

'Have you been struggling?'

Surtsey shook her head. 'Only at the start. I realise now there's no point.'

Donna walked round the bed, stopped at Surtsey's left hand. She stroked her palm with her fingertips and Surtsey let her. She checked the rope was tight, peered at the marks underneath.

'You're going to hurt yourself doing that.'

Surtsey tried not to think of the butter knife under the mattress, six inches away from Donna's hand.

Donna went to the top of the bed and lifted it, slid it against the wall.

'That's better now.'

She went to the bags and began unpacking. More clothes, fruit and veg, crisps and nuts, two large bottles of Coke.

'That's my one vice, I have to drink full-fat Coke, can't stand the diet stuff.'

Surtsey waited until Donna was leaning away placing the bottles on the floor then slid her fingertips under the mattress. The knife wasn't there. She moved her hand down along the edge of the frame but came up against nothing. The she moved it the other way, felt the metal handle of it and almost cried out. She flicked her fingers out and rested her hand on the mattress as Donna straightened up.

Surtsey breathed deeply a few times. 'How did this all start?'

Donna paused with a bag of apples in her hand. 'How do you mean?'

'I was wondering while you were away. How long has this been going on? How long have you been...' she tried to think of the right thing to say '...looking out for me?'

Donna looked at her, then out the window. She put the apples down on the table and stared at them. She looked around the table and Surtsey thought she'd spotted the missing knife. She sat on the bench and picked at the edge of the table with her fingernails.

'You really never noticed me at school, did you?'

'Of course I did.'

Donna gave her a sideways look, just a glance then away. 'That's OK, I didn't expect you to back then. You were the year above and you always hung out with the cooler girls.'

'I do remember you.'

'You're very kind, but you've already made it perfectly clear you don't remember any of the times you helped me. That's OK, I was shy and forgettable.' She smiled. 'You were very noticeable.'

'I didn't feel that way.'

'You were. Even your name, so exotic. And the way you carried yourself around the place, down the corridors, in the lunch hall, the playground. So confident. I was jealous of your confidence.'

'It was all show. No teenage girl really feels confident.'

'I'm sure that's not true.'

'Trust me, I had all the same shit going on in my head as everyone else in that place. Confidence is an illusion.'

Donna shook her head.

Surtsey kept her eyes on Donna. 'I don't know who you think I am, but I'm not that person. You don't know me.'

Donna rubbed her hands together. 'But I do, I know you better than you know yourself.'

It was Surtsey's turn to shake her head. 'This isn't about school. School was years ago. I never saw you for years until Mum went into St Columba's.'

Donna nodded. 'Do you believe in fate? Serendipity?'

'You make your own fate.'

Donna pressed her lips together. 'You're wrong. The universe throws people together, shows you the way forward. That's what happened the day Louise came to the hospice. My dad had just died three days before. I recognised you straight away and it all came back, how much I admired you at school. Maybe even worshipped you. I always assumed you'd moved away somewhere exotic, but here you were back in Joppa with the rest of us.'

'So this started with Mum?'

'I realised how much we had in common,' Donna said. 'I had just lost my mum and dad and you were losing your mum too. We were taking care of Louise together. You were so kind to her, so generous with your time. Not like your sister.'

'Everyone deals with stuff differently,' Surtsey said.

'She's a selfish cow and part of me hopes I gave her too big a dose back at your house.'

Surtsey waited a moment. 'I still don't understand. About your ... interest in me.'

Donna got up, animated. 'We're the same, don't you see? We were so different at school I could never have been your friend, but people change, Sur, that's what I've come to realise. People change. Some for the better, some for the worse. Some people become more confident, some less so. Some people deal with grief well, others run away and hide. But everything I saw of you at the hospice, every time you visited, I realised we were becoming closer, we were becoming so similar, dealing with your mum the way we did, looking after her as a team, really, sisters in our sadness.'

Surtsey screwed up her eyes. 'But you never said anything, you never spoke to me about any of this.'

'It was obvious you felt it too,' Donna said. 'I could tell by the little conversations we had, underneath the everyday chats about your mum.'

'I don't remember it like that.'

'You were telling me all about your life,' Donna said, pacing up and down. 'You were inviting me in.'

'I wasn't.'

'You just didn't know it. You needed a guardian angel and I was ready to step up.'

'I didn't need anyone spying on me.'

'I wasn't spying, I was looking out for you.'

'You spied on me with Tom.'

Donna smiled. 'I didn't find out about Tom initially. I used to watch you with Brendan, leaving work together, going out on dates. The time you gave him a blowjob on the beach when you thought no one was around. I saw you hanging out with Halima and Iona in the Espy. Then one day I followed you from King's Buildings on your own and you took a detour to a hotel on Waterloo Place. I was surprised, you didn't seem like someone with secrets and yet there you were, meeting Tom behind his family's back.'

'Don't bring his family into this.'

'You've destroyed them, you know that? You didn't think of them when you were fucking Tom.'

'I didn't mean to hurt anyone,' Surtsey said. 'I didn't want anyone to find out but you made sure they did when you killed him.'

'I couldn't stand to see you throw your life away on that man. You weren't going to end it, you didn't have the strength. And he wasn't going to either, he was just a man following his dick around. I had to be strong, I had to end it, for both of us.'

Surtsey tried to keep her voice steady. 'There's no "us".'

'Of course there is,' Donna said. 'We're here, aren't we?'

'Because you've kidnapped me and tied me up.'

Donna reached into the rucksack. 'You'll understand one day.' She pulled out a bottle of clear liquid and a facecloth. She unscrewed the lid, held the cloth over the bottle and tipped it upside down for a couple of seconds then placed the bottle on the table and came over to the bed.

'What the fuck are you doing?' Surtsey said. 'Stay away from me.'

'You need to rest,' Donna said. 'Getting worked up like this isn't good for you.'

She went to the top of the bed so that Surtsey had to arch her neck to see her. She brought the cloth down to Surtsey's face. Surtsey twisted her neck, turned her head away, but Donna held her head against the pillow as the other hand pressed the facecloth over her nose and mouth. She struggled but felt it taking her over. Her lungs were saturated and the energy disappeared from her arms and legs. Her head slumped under Donna's hand. She felt dizzy and sick, clouds filling her mind, then she dissolved into nothing.

44

A shooting pain in her calf woke her. Cramp. She grunted, tried to move her hands towards her leg, felt the rope cut into her raw wrists. She turned her ankle round in slow circles, stretching the muscles in her legs, easing the tension. Gradually the cramp subsided as she breathed heavily through her nose.

She looked up. Out the window the sky was pale blue, stretching darker to the west. She guessed it was just before dawn.

She thought about her phone. Donna said she'd sent texts to Hal and Iona. Surely they wouldn't just take one message on face value, surely they would get in touch after everything that had happened. She thought about the police, the way Donna had set her up. How she was going to finish it with the tip-offs.

She thought about Tom's face caved in. Brendan too. Her mum's rubbery skin in that back room at the hospice. All of it down to Donna.

She took in the room and spotted Donna lying in a sleeping bag on the floor between the door and the water bottles.

Surtsey watched her for a long time. Her chest was rising and falling slowly, a rasp from her nose as she breathed out. Her hands were placed together under her cheek and her knees were pulled up towards her chest. The skin on her face was slack and she looked carefree.

Surtsey felt with her left hand for the knife under the mattress, keeping her eyes on Donna. She got her fingers on the handle and lifted it out. Holding it upside down in her palm, with the handle at the inside of her knuckle and the blade pointing down towards her wrist, she placed it against the rope there and began a gentle sawing motion. The rope wasn't thick, standard camping cord, but it was probably strong. The knife started making inroads into the material.

Donna made a snuffling noise like a pig at a trough.

Surtsey stopped and waited.

The knife was hidden in her palm, so even if Donna woke she might not notice it unless Surtsey was caught in the act of cutting. She felt sweat on her brow as she moved the knife against the rope. The edge of the material had frayed, it was working. She kept going, propelled by the idea that she could free herself.

Then what? Look for her phone or run for it? The boat had to be somewhere. She'd glimpsed the jetty out of the door when Donna left before and it seemed empty. Wherever the boat was she would find it, the island wasn't that big. She would find the boat, get back to shore and this would be over.

Donna coughed and rubbed at her nose with the back of her hand. Surtsey froze. Donna's hand went under her cheek and she moaned, wriggled her shoulders into the sleeping bag.

Surtsey breathed three times, slow and easy, then began sawing again. More frayed ends of material came away, tiny yellow strands. She stopped and put pressure on the rope, tried to push her wrist through it. Didn't budge.

She went back to cutting, methodical, up and down, concentrating, her eyes on Donna, glancing down at the rope at her wrist and seeing more strands come away.

She stopped and pushed against the material again. It strained but didn't break. She tried again. Same.

Back to cutting. Come on you stupid fucking knife, do your work.

Donna shifted her hips inside the sleeping bag and Surtsey heard a fart.

She closed her eyes for a moment, felt her heart thump in her rib cage, as loud as thunder in her ears.

She opened her eyes and slid the knife against the rope again. Slow, methodical, then faster, more frantic as threads spiralled away from the knot. She stopped and tensed her arm, pulled it towards her, felt the burn of the rope against her skin, blood where it was raw.

She pulled again and her hand jerked a few inches as she felt the rope slacken. She heaved her arm again. The rope was looser now but there was still resistance. She examined it. It was cut through in one place but still tangled. If she could get her fingers into the frayed ends maybe she could separate the strands and free her arm. She placed the knife under the mattress, keeping watch on Donna across the room. Then she dug her fingers in to the half-knot at the inside of her wrist. She tugged and pulled but it was awkward, her fingers doubled back to her wrist, pain across the sinews of her hand as she strained. But it was loosening. She dug her forefinger into a gap that had widened between strands and hooked the top strand clear, and the rest fell away leaving just a pile of rope around the bed frame, her arm completely free.

She raised her hand in the air, flexed her fingers to shake the cramp away, twisted and stretched her arm about.

Then a noise. The plate on the table rattled, the water bottles juddered on the floor. Another fucking earthquake, Jesus. The bed shook, vibrations through her spine and legs. Donna shuffled in her sleeping bag. Surtsey grabbed the loose rope and draped a strand over her wrist, leaving her arm on the bed as if it was still tied up. This was a bigger quake, more than a tremor. Donna's eyes opened and she clambered to her hands and knees. The walls seemed to breathe in and out, the table shuddered towards Donna, bumping into the bench. The bed inched away from the wall again as the water pan clattered from the stove onto the floor.

Donna stared at Surtsey the whole time. It took everything for Surtsey not to lift her arm up and cover her face as masonry dust fell from a crack in the wall to her right. The corrugated iron roof bent and flexed like a squeezebox, everything about the bothy suddenly transient, transforming from stable shelter to death trap.

And it kept going. Christ, this was big. A clatter and thud outside sounded like rock fall and Surtsey wondered how close it was to the hut. She imagined being crushed by a tumbling volcanic plug, all evidence of everything Donna had done flattened to nothing, the two of them included.

Donna was crouching on her knees, narrow eyes on Surtsey. No point in trying to stand up, she would only fall. Surtsey glanced at the rope over her left wrist, prayed it wouldn't shake loose and drop. The bed was still vibrating, its legs chattering on the floor. One of the water bottles tumbled over followed by another, as the pile of clothes on the table flopped to the ground too.

Then stillness. The walls back to being walls, the roof still over their heads, the ground solid again.

Donna stood. 'Wow.'

Surtsey puffed her cheeks and raised her eyebrows.

Donna went to the window and looked out.

'That sounded like a landslide,' she said, turning back.

She looked around the room at the stuff on the floor, the spread of water from the pan turned on its side next to the stove.

'I'll sort this in a minute,' she said. 'Better look outside first, check the building.'

She strode over to the door and left, letting it clatter behind her.

Surtsey pulled at the knots on her right wrist with her left hand, digging her nails between the strands, loosening them, but it was tight, several knots at once and her fingers and arm muscles ached. Blood ran down her forearm from her wrist as she worked. She was breathing hard, glancing at the door every few seconds. Eventually she dug a piece of rope free then the rest became easier. She whipped one strand then another up and out, until she had a last crossover to undo. She untied it and shook her hand free then sat up and began working on her legs.

Her ankles were tied separately, two knots to undo. She started on the left one first, easier now with both hands free, pulling at the ropes, unhooking the interlaced strands, fumbling for a second before getting the last knot undone and moving to her other ankle. Same again, hands trembling with the effort and exhaustion, fumbling for the free end of the rope, pushing it through, flicking the end up and away, then repeating, feeling the pressure release on her ankle as the rope fell away and she was free.

The door opened and Donna came in. She stood for a second in the doorway. Surtsey swung her legs over the side of the bed and stood up. Donna ran at her, grabbing her around the waist as the pair of them tumbled to the floor between the bed and the table. Surtsey had the air knocked out of her lungs, her chest crushed under Donna's weight. She tried to prise Donna off but her arms were weak, so she heaved and rolled the pair of them together until Donna bumped against a table leg. She got an arm free and grabbed Donna's hair, yanked it up and slammed her head against the floor, a spray of saliva from Donna's mouth into Surtsey's face. Donna surged upward, smashing her forehead into Surtsey's teeth and nose, blood spurting from her face. Surtsey lifted a knee into Donna's groin then threw a fist into her stomach and felt Donna's arms release her grip. She threw another jab at her face, felt the bone in Donna's cheek crack, or maybe it was the bone in her own hand. She scrambled upright using the table edge as leverage and stumbled towards the door.

'Bitch,' Donna said behind her.

Surtsey staggered to the door and grabbed the handle, using it to keep herself up. She glanced back and saw Donna getting up, spitting on the floor, holding her face.

She flung the door open and ran.

45

She thrust one foot in front of the other, putting everything she had into it, getting up speed, increasing the distance between her and the bothy. She heard the door slam behind her as she sprinted, lungs already burning, calves and thighs straining, arms pumping as she gulped for air.

She was heading downhill, the momentum throwing her towards the jetty. She had to keep her eyes on the ground over this terrain, rocky and jagged, holes everywhere, impossible to judge it well, clambering and clattering over patches of rubble and around boulders. She glanced at the jetty a hundred yards away but couldn't see any boat. Maybe it was tied up round the other side.

She stumbled, lost her balance as a shower of scree slid beneath her foot. She put a hand out and scraped her palm on a jutting rock. She looked behind, her pulse raging, breath wheezing. Donna was coming after her, a hundred yards away, holding a hammer.

She started off again towards the jetty.

'Please be there,' she said between gasps of air. 'Please.'

She leapt over more bulbous rocks and found a stretch of level land, sand in a wide crevice, and picked up speed as she approached the jetty. The sand under her feet was more reliable than rocks but it sapped the strength from her legs, pockets of deep stuff slowing her down.

Donna was still behind, grimace on her face, hammer clutched in her fist.

Surtsey had a few more yards in the deep sand then she was at the jetty. She pitched round the blind side and stared along its length.

No boat.

She looked at Donna, still a distance away, then out to sea. Maybe it was anchored further out. But why would Donna do that if she had to bring supplies ashore? Didn't make sense. It had to be pulled up on the shore somewhere else. Maybe she didn't want it at the jetty in case anyone saw.

Donna was gaining fast. Surtsey had to move. She had to find the boat, but which way? Up the coast towards the research site or double back to the right, around the hut to the cove where she'd found Tom?

Donna was almost on her. So close that Surtsey could hear her breathing.

She checked one more time along the length of the jetty then turned back.

Donna was smiling, thirty yards away.

The cove.

Surtsey began running but only got a few yards when the ground shook violently, throwing her forwards. She staggered on but another jolt made the earth come up to meet her feet before she expected, and she tipped onto her knees. Three more huge shudders threw her onto her back as the ground shifted and grumbled. Another earthquake. Much, much bigger than any of the previous ones. There was a massive bang and crack, a noise Surtsey had never heard before, that resonated through her body. She shuffled backwards and propped herself up on her elbows, looked back. Donna was lying on her stomach in the sand, looking around, holding onto the earth as if it was the last solid thing in the universe. But it wasn't solid at all.

Beyond Donna's prostrate body a cascade of rocks were tumbling down the hillside from higher up, heading east of them towards the cliffs. The noise of the boulders tumbling over each other was excruciating, she felt it in her gut and bowels. She looked further up the slope. Smoke was shooting out both volcanic vents, billowing clouds of it, as the earth continued to shake and judder, throwing her around.

Then a crack and a growl of pure power, something deep beneath them but all around them too. The saddle of land between the vents exploded into the air, huge plumes of debris flying into the blue sky, rock and dust and smoke. Through it all, Surtsey saw red.

Lava. The Inch was erupting.

'Jesus Christ.'

Thin ash was already falling around them as the earth shook, a giant crack appearing from the remains of the western vent, spreading downhill like a lightning bolt, cutting solid rock and prising it apart, reaching its fingers down to the scientific hut which was torn in two like freshly-baked bread.

Crimson lava sprayed into the air high above the peaks, thicker rivers of the stuff leeching over the lips of the vents and slurping towards them.

Surtsey saw Donna lift her head and look behind. She turned back and they held each other's gaze for a few seconds, as if sharing this unstoppable moment.

Donna wiped ash and sand from her eyes and pushed herself onto her knees.

The earth gave another series of shrugs but she didn't lose balance.

Surtsey saw another crack jolt into existence behind Donna, one side lifting suddenly to make a giant step a hundred feet long and ten feet high, dust and sand and rocks falling in the chasm between, sliding into the bowels of the earth.

Donna said something while looking at her, but all Surtsey could hear was the rumble and thrum of the earth and the volcano erupting and rocks falling.

She lurched to her feet as another jolt burst through the ground, throwing her off kilter.

Donna was on her feet as well.

Lava sped down the hillside in their direction, two hundred yards away. Dust and ash filled the air, black and grey, coating everything, stinging Surtsey's eyes, settling in her hair. The sulphur stench of rotten eggs was everywhere. Stones thudded into the sand from above, and more rocks bounced down the slopes further up, heading east.

'It's over,' Surtsey said. 'Look around.'

Donna didn't take her eyes off Surtsey, just stared, shaking her head.

Surtsey began to run round the coast.

The ash cloud towered over the island now, cloaking them in

darkness. The sky behind was still blue in the east where the sun would be coming up soon above Berwick Law. But overhead was blackness, dark snow falling over the land, clogging her nose and throat. Surtsey tried to pick her way over the rocks but more tremors threw her balance every few seconds. It had been going on so long now it felt like the world would never be stable again.

A boulder bounced down the hill to her left, clipping the edge of the torn bothy and crushing one wall to nothing. It bounded on, five, six bounces then tumbled into the sea. Surtsey turned to see Donna getting closer, then she set off again, trying to find the hard, smooth ground she needed to get her speed up. But the judders kept coming, and now she saw a lava flow spreading westward, a river throbbing down the hill from the nearest vent, red pushing through the black crust as it tumbled over itself. Up above, sparks and ash were still spilling into the sky, volcanic lightning bolts dancing inside the towering black cloud.

The earth still shook, the equilibrium of the land shifting one way then the other. Surtsey lost her balance as she clambered around more rocks then found the bottom end of the crevice that had split the hut in two. She ran to the narrowest point and jumped, just a couple of feet but the fissure into darkness beneath made her sweat.

Her eyes and nose stung and she coughed up dirt from her lungs as she heaved more air in, tried to catch breath. She looked behind and Donna was still following, it was easier for her, able to follow in the path Surtsey had cleared.

Surtsey ran on, soft sand under her feet now sucking at her ankles. She kicked along, the beach to her right frothing and slapping against the shore. The earth tilted and the slab of land she was on swung upwards to her left, pushing her towards the water which flipped up and slapped the land in retaliation.

Visibility was low now as Surtsey rounded the corner into the cove. Thick ash rained down on everything, bloody rivers cascading down the steep corrie surrounding the cove. She had a flash of Tom's body lying over there, the gulls pecking at his eyes, then she stumbled and fell, smacking her temple against a jagged rock, blood dripping onto the sand. She wiped at it, dizzy, then staggered on.

She felt the air leave her lungs as Donna crashed into her from behind, a tackle to the ground, sand cramming into Surtsey's mouth and eyes as her face planted in it.

She spat and tried to shake Donna free, managed to wriggle herself onto her back, blinked the ash out of her eyes and saw Donna sitting astride her, smiling. Donna lifted the hammer in her hand and began swinging it down when a shower of scree hit her in the head, knocking her over, the hammer dropping somewhere to the side.

Surtsey staggered up, heart crashing, gasping, and turned again.

The lava was fifty yards behind and heading towards them.

She looked past it. The shape of the vents was different now, much lower and wider. Another blast of rock and dirt launched into the sky above her head, billowing upwards. The ash drifting down on her now was hot, singeing her clothes and skin, and she could feel the heat from the lava like an open oven door. She turned to look at Donna lying on the sand, then beyond that to the sea.

Then she saw it.

Her boat.

Pushed up just past the waterline in the corner of the cove. It was a few hundred yards away across a channel of clear sand, but Donna's body lay in the way. She seemed out cold, pebbles and dirt sprayed across her back. Surtsey couldn't see the hammer, but Donna's hands were empty.

Another jolt and Surtsey's knees went from under her. The land to her left sank away as if it had melted, black rock disappearing into a widening rift. The tilt of the ground threw Surtsey towards the chasm, but she righted herself and ran.

The crevice was spreading to her left, narrowing her way forward. A boulder thudded in front of her. She stepped around Donna's body but felt a hand grab her ankle and pull her to the ground. She kicked out behind, saw Donna clawing at her, the lava pouring down the hill behind them, the heat from it shimmering the air like a furnace. She kicked her other leg into Donna's face, caught her in the eye with her heel and felt the hand let go of her ankle. She scrambled backwards then dragged herself downhill, away from the lava and cracked earth, towards the beach and the boat. Another boulder thumped into the sand to her right and the ground shuddered, the air seemed to expand and contract. Surtsey stumbled and threw a hand out, pushing herself off an outcrop and downwards.

She risked a look back. Donna was running behind, head down, one foot after the other, blood streaming down her cheek.

The waves in front of Surtsey were churning with the shaking earth, slapping against the corner of the cove, splashing on the sand in random torrents. The boat was being thrown about on the shore.

Another shower of pebbles landed all about her like bullet holes in the sand, some of them striking her head and back, making her wince and throw her hands up for protection. But she didn't stop, kept running straight to the boat, heaving it into the water and kicking up spray, salty mouthfuls of it, the cold shock to her body as she waded in behind, then suddenly no ground underfoot and she was swimming, gripping the rope that ran around the side of the boat, pulling herself against the hull, flopping over the side like a landed fish.

She lay exhausted for a second trying to get her breath back, then sat up and looked back.

Donna was sitting on the edge of the beach, water slopping at her feet, ash and dust cascading all around her, huge pillars of cloud pouring from the vents at the peak of the island. The lava was fifty yards behind her and moving fast in her direction, spreading tendrils out along every path, some into the new gaping cleft to the right, some onto the sand, throwing up sparks as the sand sizzled in the heat.

'Come on,' Surtsey said, beckoning her into the water.

Donna looked at Surtsey and shook her head.

Surtsey stared. 'Get in the boat.'

Donna glanced behind her. The lava was thirty yards. Twenty. Surtsey could feel the heat from here. She reached for the starter. Another quake sent a huge rock fall tumbling away from the vent down the eastern side, and Surtsey saw a chunk of the cliffs slide into the sea. Away to her left the rocky edge of the cove crumpled like paper and fell into the water. The chasm to the right of Donna was wider, spreading to the shore then underwater. A surge of water almost tipped the boat over as Surtsey pulled on the chord and got the motor running.

She watched as Donna just sat there. The lava was fifteen yards, ten, chasing little flames of burning sand towards her. She lay down on her back just as the lava reached her and swept over her body, spreading over her like treacle, swallowing her in a few seconds before it reached the water's edge and threw plumes of white steam hissing into the air. The heat from it scalded Surtsey's face and she fell back into the boat. The stench of ammonia burned at her eyes and throat. She pulled her T-shirt over her nose and mouth and sat up. She looked at the place where Donna had been but all she could see were vivid red rivers spilling into the sea, creating billowing steam clouds that sizzled over the surface of the water then upwards.

An explosion from the highest vent threw rocks skywards, ash and black smoke everywhere, boulders and pebbles raining down all around her, thudding into the water as another quake spread the cracks in the island deeper and wider, the surging water rocking the boat.

Surtsey gunned the engine and angled the rudder in a turning circle away from the island, the noise of it thrashing behind her, the rumble of rockslides, the crash of volcanic explosions, the hiss and sizzle of lava sucked under the ocean, the steam and smoke and ash filling the sky and her senses.

She was fifty yards away now, seventy, a hundred, heading east, the most direct route away from the chaos behind her, Musselburgh and East Lothian in her sight, Portobello to the right.

She slumped back against the stern of the boat, the throbbing engine eventually drowning out the noise from the Inch. She coughed and coughed, spat black phlegm into the boat, her eyes painful, her skin raw.

She was away now, several hundred yards, halfway to the coastline and safety.

She turned back to look. The ash cloud stretched into the atmosphere, lava pumping out of the vents. The edges of the island were crumbling and slipping into the sea, new lava flows crawling over them and crashing into the boiling water.

She sat looking at it for a long time as the boat got further away. Eventually she turned and looked at the prom. Hundreds of people were on the shoreline watching the Inch tear itself apart. She steered the boat towards them.

46

Traces of high cloud in a thick blue sky. Surtsey wriggled her toes in the sand as she sat on the beach soaking up the sun. The tide was halfway out leaving stretches of wet sand, strewn with lines of seaweed, gulls and terns slapping through the wash looking for sandworms. Dog walkers were coming and going, a golden retriever lolloping towards them then away. She sat with Iona on one side and Hal on the other, the three of them silent. Fifty yards to their left an old woman stood on her own, staring out to sea. And beyond her a thin ribbon of steam rose from the water.

The Inch was gone.

It was ten days since the eruption started. It had gone on for four days, not quite as dramatic as those first few hours, less spewing lava and fewer rockslides. But the ash cloud continued, closing northern European airspace for a week. As the clouds streamed into the sky and dissipated into the upper atmosphere, the Inch was sinking. Great fissures had opened up along the fault line under the firth, and a chain of earthquakes saw the cliffs, beaches and slopes of the island gradually disappear. For several days there were fears of extreme waves, but tsunamis need space to get momentum, hours of open water to build up energy and height. It was lucky, in the end, that the firth was so enclosed. A couple of super-high tides had soaked the promenade, and in the East Neuk and North Berwick they kept people away from the shore for a day or two, but no real damage was done. Except to the Inch.

Surtsey stared at the thread of white linking the sea to the sky. It was a calm day, the steam lazy in the heat.

'You OK?' Hal said.

Surtsey turned and smiled. 'I'm fine.'

Hal handed her the hash pipe and lighter and she inhaled. Just a little, her lungs were still delicate. She passed it to Iona who sucked on it in silence.

Surtsey had spent two nights in hospital. Concussion from a knock to the head, burns to her face and hands, the ankle and wrist cuts from being restrained, lots more cuts and bruises, plus severe smoke inhalation.

Once she was considered fit to leave there were two full days at the police station answering questions. The concussion hadn't damaged her memory, so she gave as clear an account as she could of everything that happened on the island and before.

Yates and Flannery were highly sceptical. It was a bit too handy that the person responsible for the murders was dead at the bottom of the ocean, literally petrified, along with all the evidence. So they kept asking and Surtsey kept telling them. The fact that she told the whole truth for the first time, including finding Tom's body, helped. She couldn't get her story mixed up because it was true.

And the evidence began to back her up. The police didn't have Surtsey's phone, or Tom's or Donna's, but they got records for all three and the calls and messages bore out what Surtsey told them.

Once they began looking into Donna Jones more evidence appeared. She disappeared at the time of the eruption, just as Surtsey explained, and hadn't turned up for work. The police got a warrant to search her house and found medical supplies taken from the hospice plus receipts for boat hire that matched the date of Tom's murder. They also found notebooks full of Surtsey's movements and Donna's own ramblings. There was a heap to go through, but the initial impression was one of unhinged obsession.

Once they knew to look for Donna, they found more. She was spotted in CCTV footage taken from King's Buildings, close to the Grant Institute at the right time for Brendan's death. Surtsey told them about Tom's boat at Fisherrow, how Donna was going to plant DNA evidence in it. They found the boat there right enough, and when they checked the harbour security footage there was Donna, taking her hire boat out on the evening of Tom's death and returning with Tom's boat in tow later on. They found hair samples from Surtsey in a small bag on Tom's boat, she hadn't planted it yet. They also found Surtsey's hair on the quartz that killed Brendan, clumsily planted according to forensics.

And there was the drugged wine, plus Iona and Hal's evidence. Two empty bottles showed traces of diazepam in large quantities. Iona and Hal couldn't remember much, but they spoke of feeling unwell and being helped to bed by Donna. By the time they woke up Surtsey was in hospital and the Inch was on fire.

The police requested a post mortem of Louise. The embalmers hadn't done her yet at the funeral home so she was cut open and tested, and there were large amounts of morphine in her system. It didn't prove Donna had killed her or forced her to take them, that would always be unknown. Surtsey would never know if her mum wanted to die when she did.

She looked at the box in her lap. The funeral director called it an ashes casket, but that seemed too fancy for a simple wooden box.

Iona reached across Surtsey and handed the pipe back to Halima.

The three of them hadn't really talked about what happened. What could they say? Iona and Hal had eventually received garbled phone messages from a concussed Surtsey to say she was at hospital and the police wanted to speak to her. Groggy themselves, they went to visit and she explained what Donna had done as best she could.

The police were still investigating and Surtsey wasn't off the hook, but Donna was the focus of their enquiries. How that would work in terms of the law, Surtsey had no idea. She had no wish to keep in touch with the cops and was trying to forget the whole thing.

But of course they could never forget. Surtsey looked at Iona. They hadn't spoken about their mum's letter. Again, what else was there to say? Iona had just learned her dad was dead along with their mum. And that she had two half-sisters. The police had apparently informed Alice that Donna was their prime suspect now. Surtsey wondered if that made any difference in the face of her grief. And they told her about Louise's letter too, that her girls had a half-sister. That her dead husband had been lying to her their whole marriage. Surtsey tried to picture a future where Iona would have a relationship with Alice's girls, but she couldn't conjure anything up.

She ran a finger along the edge of the box. They had the funeral three days ago, after all the post-mortem stuff, then picked up the ashes from the home this morning.

This had been the plan all along, Louise had told her. No details for the funeral, she didn't care about any of that, but she wanted her ashes scattered in the sea, here in the Firth of Forth.

Surtsey looked over again at the steam, the only sign that anything was still happening under the surface of the water. The only indication there had ever been an island out there, a piece of land she'd presumed would be there forever. But nothing is forever, nothing is truly reliable.

At the bottom of Bath Street, Bastian and the New Thule protestors had been having a combined party and wake since the eruption started. At first they were joyful that their god or whoever was speaking to them, then when it became apparent the Inch was sinking they were distraught. But then they turned it around in their minds like a resurrection thing, a new Inch would come soon.

But Surtsey's island was gone.

'Shall we do this?' she said.

She turned to Hal then Iona, who both nodded.

They stood up, brushing sand from their clothes. Surtsey felt the grass make her head spin, but she didn't mind.

The three of them walked to the water's edge, hesitated for a moment, looking at each other. Surtsey reached out a hand to Iona who took it. She had her mum tucked under her other arm.

They walked into the water, the cold making Surtsey shiver. They kept going, up to their knees, over their thighs until it was at their waists.

Surtsey waited a moment, letting her body acclimatise to the cold, then dropped Iona's hand and held the casket in both hands.

'Do you want to?' she said to Iona.

Iona shook her head. 'You do it.'

Surtsey felt Halima's hand on her back.

She opened the lid. Just a pile of grey dust, small clumps amongst finer stuff, the same colour as the sand on the Inch, or the ash that rained down in the middle of it all. That's all we were in the end, just dust.

She lowered the box to the water, stuck her hand in and scooped the remains into the sea. She dug down, feeling it under her fingernails, scraping at the unvarnished wood. She looked at Iona and Hal who were watching her.

Eventually she'd scooped out all she could, so she submerged the box under the water, ran her thumb and fingers around the inside. She lifted the box out and upturned it, the last few drops of grainy water dripping into the sea.

The ashes disappeared in a stream past Iona, gone in a few seconds, then they were just standing in the sea in their clothes with an empty box.

'Let's go,' Surtsey said.

They turned and waded out of the water, arms around each other, heading for home.

Acknowledgements

Immense thanks to Karen Sullivan for taking a chance on me, and to everyone else at Orenda Books for their passion and encouragement. Thanks to my agent, Phil Patterson, for his huge enthusiasm and support. And the biggest thanks to Tricia, Aidan and Amber, as always.